PETTY IN PINK

PETTY IN PINK

a POSEUR novel

by Rachel Maude

Illustrations by Rachel Maude
Do-it-yourself patterns by Compai

poppy

LITTLE, BROWN AND COMPANY
New York   Boston

Poppy

Little, Brown and Company
Hachette Book Group
237 Park Avenue, New York, NY 10017
For more of your favorite series, go to www.pickapoppy.com

Poppy is an imprint of Little, Brown and Company.
The Poppy name and logo are trademarks of Hachette Book Group, Inc.

First Edition: August 2009

The Poppy name and logo are trademarks of Hachette Book Group

ISBN 978-0-316-06585-6

10 9 8 7 6 5 4 3 2 1

CWO

Printed in the United States of America

Book design by Tracy Shaw

To ma clique:
Annie "Kashi" Baker
Jamie "JayJay" Lawrence
and
Crow "Tom" Meaney

Charlotte Beverwil balances boyfriend school and career...

Janie Finnish

The Girl: Charlotte Beverwil
The Getup: Skirt and top by Valentino, shoes by Christian
Louboutin, crocheted cashmere cowl "by moi, thank you"

Bonjour! It's Friday morning at Winston Prep. Okay, fine. It's
Friday morning a smackload of other places, too — but do we
really want to start our day at your mama's house? No, we don't.
We want to start here, at Winston, the *exclusivicious* private high
school in the Hollywood Hills and so-called stomping ground of
the young, rich, and phatuous. Not that girls here stomp — not
if they want to stay standing. In their Fendi flats, Blahnik booties,
and precarious Prada pumps, the best they can do is teeter-totter,
clitter-clatter, and — on occasion — pitter-patter. Mere stomping they leave to the Ugg-clad masses.

Every Friday is sweet — the promise of Saturday unfurls into
the air, like a baking birthday cake behind closed doors — *but this
Friday's sweeter,* Charlotte Beverwil smiled, directing her gleaming,
cream-colored 1969 Jaguar into her coveted Showroom parking
spot. Allowing a quick glance into her gold-rimmed rearview, she
feigned cool obliviousness to the fifty or so stares firmly fixed in
the direction of her ruby taillights. As Winston's only outdoor
parking lot, the Showroom, as it had been nicknamed long ago,
was all about "see and be seen," and with her tumultuous long dark
hair, flickering chlorine green gaze, and perfect too-tiny body (the

girl was like supermodel bonsai), you can bet your bottom trust fund Charlotte was more than just watched.

She was worshipped.

The heavy Jaguar door swung open, all buttery tan leather, polished walnut accents, and in the side pocket, the glossy top half of the latest French *Vogue* — a glimpse of well-oiled interior that served as backdrop for the main event: a gorgeous gray suede asymmetrical strap stiletto pump. The size six four-inch heeler hit the pavement, followed *tout de suite* by its mate, and then: step, step, pivot, *slam*.

She'd barely been out of the car three seconds when her two best friends, Kate Joliet and Laila Pikser, materialized in two fragrant bursts of Chanel Coco Mademoiselle. "Oh-oo-o-oo-oh!" Laila whinnied like a pony stranded in the rain. A wing of burnished copper hair swept across her high, Elizabethan forehead, skimming her clear mascara-lacquered lashes. "You look so puh-*retty*."

"I know," Charlotte frowned, smoothing her high-waisted gathered skirt in lustrous navy silk. A sheer gray cashmere top clung to her delicate arms, gathering into curling, cabbage-like layers at her throat and cascading in thick frills down the front. "The question is . . ." She placed her hands on her hips, tilted her china cup chin, and faced her friends at a saucy three-quarter angle. "Do I look profesh?"

"Omigod, *très*," Kate assured her, her underfed fox-face awash with envy. Smoothing her platinum Agyness Deyn pixie cut with a bony-fingered lavender-polished hand, she sighed. "I wish I had a business meeting to go to."

"I know, right?" Laila pouted, unsnapped her brass-studded Balenciaga tote, and stared inside — as though deep within its black canvas–lined depths commenced the business meeting to which *she*, not Charlotte, was invited. "You are so lucky."

"You guys make it sound like I'm not working," Charlotte chastised them in her best no-nonsense tone. Never mind her non-sensical heart, pumping giddiness into her veins until they fizzed like soda straws. "Do you even know how hard it is to balance school, a boyfriend, *and* a *career?*"

Wheee! She'd always wanted to say that.

Last weekend, her original designer brand, Poseur, made the leap from negligible *non* to absolute *on*, and all in the time it takes to say "nice to meet you." Like a tangled Diane von Furstenberg dress, it was hard to wrap her mind around, especially when she remembered Poseur began with a Winston elective called (of all humiliating things) The Trend Set. When she'd learned she'd been enrolled, *against her will*, in a class with Melissa "Me-Me" Moon, Petra "Petri Dish" Greene, and Janie "Pompidou" Farrish — three people with whom she had *nothing* in common — she was *not* beside herself ("beside herself" was where everyone wanted to be), but *far away from herself* in despair. And nothing, not even Yves Saint Laurent himself descending from heaven for the express purpose of saying "zaire, zaire," would console her. And if Yves had gone further? If he had, for instance, declared, "Togezaire, you and zeeze gayrls will create zee fabulous fashion!" she would have replied, "Whatever, Yves. Lay off the angel dust."

But she'd be wrong.

Case in point? Winston's premier couture handbag, the Trick-or-Treater, had been discovered by Ted Pelligan, the larger-than-life fashion luminary behind such exclusive retail wonderlands as Ted Pelligan: Beverly Hills, and Ted Pelligan: Santa Monica. Simply put, Ted Pelligan was more than *just a person*; he was an *institution*. And you can't spell institution without *the* most fashionable word in the English language.

In.

Now, in just a matter of nine hours, Charlotte and her courtiers in couture — 1) Melissa Moon, Duchess of Diva, 2) Petra Greene, Princess of PC, and 3) Her Royal Shyness Janie Farrish — would depart from their peach stucco and wrought-iron school gates, wind into the dappled shade of Coldwater Canyon, sail down sunny Sunset Boulevard, hang a right on Crescent Heights, and meet their destiny/destination: Ted Pelligan: Melrose, *the Ted Pelligan flagship store*. Janie's mother had made the call last week, setting up the four o'clock appointment, but apart from the dreary time-and-place details had gathered no clues as to what the four girls should expect. "He definitely wants to carry the handbag though, right?" Melissa had urgently checked. "Did he say we should dress up, or is it more, like, business casual?" Charlotte had wondered. "Will we have to drop out of school?" Petra had hopefully inquired. "Did he even sound *excited*?" Janie had blurted at last. "Do you really think he's, like, *serious* about this?"

"I think that's the point of this meeting, girls," Mrs. Farrish had patiently replied, clapping Janie's cell phone shut and blinking behind her funky turquoise cat-eye glasses. "You can ask all your questions then."

To say the week passed slowly was an understatement of the first degree.

At the Jag's smooth fender, Kate and Laila arranged their ballet bodies into languid positions of repose, and Charlotte scanned the increasingly bustling Showroom floor. Metallic luxury cars poured through the main gate, tooled around the boisterous crowd for empty spots, or headed — dejected — to park underground. Popular upperclassmen clambered aboard already-parked car hoods, chattering like penguins on tricked-out ice floes, or nodding solemnly to the boom-boom-*thump* of competing bass lines. United as they were in Poseur, Charlotte and her three partners belonged to entirely different social scenes, congregating on opposite corners of the lot: spotting them was no easy task. She just about abandoned her search when two bright beamers squeezed past each other, bumpers parting to reveal a flashy platinum Lexus convertible — not to mention its equally flashy owner. Whipping a yard-long, black-as-licorice braid over her right shoulder, she popped the trunk and bent over.

Her bedazzled badonkadonk glittered in the sun.

"No!" Charlotte cried, plunging a manicured hand into her classic black satin Lanvin tote. Kate and Laila sprang from the Jag and trotted to her side, but Charlotte only shook her head, uprooted her vintage gray-and-red Dior sunglasses, and clattered them to her face. Sharing a wondering look, her friends slipped on their matching white titanium Ditas and, together with Charlotte, returned their nonglare-impaired stares to the platinum Lexus. They blinked once, gasped.

"No!"

For the first professional appointment of her career, Poseur Public Relations Director Melissa Moon had paired a black corset top with a cropped black, gold, and cream Chanel tweed jacket, black matte satin skinny pants, black Jimmy Choo stilettos, and classic antique-white pearls. It was the kind of chic, understated ensemble socialite-cum-designer Tory Burch might wear — except while Tory kept her pearls around her *neck*, Melissa had hers studded on her *ass* — and in no random order, either.

"Kiss it," Charlotte read aloud in trembling disbelief. "It actually says 'kiss it'!"

"But . . ." Laila crumpled her heart-shaped face like a day-old valentine. "Kiss what?"

"Her bootie," Kate sighed, fluttering her clear gray eyes shut. "Obvie."

"We're supposed to look like *career* women," Charlotte whimpered, burying her face in her Jo Malone orange blossom–scented hands. "Not . . ."

"*Rear* women?" Kate offered, knitting her dark brown eyebrows for comic effect. Charlotte glared: so not funny.

"It could be worse," Laila pointed out, hoping to deflect attention from her earlier cluelessness. "She could be dressed like *that*."

On the opposite side of the parking lot, Petra Greene laughingly slipped from the torn sky-blue vinyl backseat of Joaquin Whitman's custom-painted VW (aka VD) bus, a pair of tiny circular Hendrix-style purple shades — the cheapo generic ones sold on Venice Beach — shielding her wide-set tea-colored eyes. Her sleep-tousled, waist-length honey-gold hair was held in place by some kind of blue silk print bandanna two shades darker than her frayed denim cutoffs, all of which she dared to pair with a shrunken pinstriped tuxedo jacket. She stretched like a cat, arching her back, hands high in the air. The cracked white letters on her faded green cotton t-shirt read: RE-use. RE-duce. RE-cycle.

"Uch," Kate scoffed. "RE-*dic*. And is that a Paul Smith *tie* on her *forehead*?"

"It must be cutting off circulation to her brain," Laila noted with genuine concern. "Why else would she dress like that?"

"Today of all days," Kate returned.

"Do either of you have a light?" Charlotte intruded, lifting a gold-tipped Gauloise to her Parisian pout. Kate gasped, slapping the contraband from her best friend's slender fingertips. The resigned brunette watched the Gauloise pinwheel through the air and land with a bounce on the pavement, crushed within moments by an unsuspecting silver Barneys CO-OP gladiator sandal. She sighed.

"About that Calculus quiz!" Kate barked loudly, darting her paranoid gaze in all directions. Laila froze, eyeing the mutilated cigarette like a ticking bomb.

"Hello," the scandalized redhead squeezed out in a hiss. "We are at *school*?"

"Well, I'm having a total meltdown," Charlotte explained with a shrug, the twin surfaces of her chlorine irises unruffled as indoor pools. "Isn't that obvie?"

"Maybe you should try deep breathing," suggested Kate, standing between the culprit and her smoking gun.

"Les ha-ha," she scoffed, turning the beaten gold bangle on her delicate wrist. "I might as well *smoke air.*"

"Maybe you could just ask them to change?" Laila ventured.

"No," Charlotte scowled. Last time she calmly suggested Melissa "might want to cover up a little," the ghetto diva flashed, "Cover up? As in the cover-up you'll need when I go Chris Brown on your ass?" Last time she told Petra to take a shower (the girl had *honey* in her hair), the hippie goddess only smiled. *Ugh!* They were insufferable. "What I need to do," she resumed, pressing her manicured fingers to her temples. Her greenish blue eyes fluttered shut. "Is think."

Kate and Laila nibbled their Nars-lacquered nails and shared a fretful glance. They really, really hated it when Charlotte thought; on the list of activities to which they could *not* relate, "thinking" topped the list. Of course, a close second arrived in that other incomprehensible commitment. *Poseur.* If she'd wanted to start a fashion label, then why hadn't she started one with *them?* Charlotte explained it hadn't been her choice; Miss Paletsky, Winston's sweet-tempered if Dracula-voiced Special Studies adviser, had all but forced her to join, and now it was *way* too late to drop — that is, not without a gaping hole in her record. *Fine,* they granted. But if that was the *whole* reason, then why take the label so *seriously?* Why care so deeply how her associates dressed, if indeed "associate" remained the accurate term? Janie Farrish, that pathetic pimple, seemed suspiciously close to "friend." "Oh, puh-lease," Charlotte had retorted. "She's not a *friend*, she's a *project* — like a dilapidated Tuscan villa you fix up for fun and sell when you're bored." Except (and this is what kept them up at night), what if Charlotte never *got* bored? What if she decided she *liked* her Tuscan villa? What if she moved the hell *in?* The preliminary signs were there: she'd asked Janie to sit with them at Town

Meeting, Winston's *very* public school assembly; she found *totally* random ways to drop her name into conversation; once, she'd even invited her to *lunch*. At *Kate Mantellini*. With them! "Well, we'd had work to discuss," she'd explained, exasperated. *Yeah, right,* they'd thought, bobbing their well-groomed eyebrows. Like a raggedy red rag thrown into pure white laundry, "work" had slowly but effectively bled into "life," turning it an unsightly and *deeply* icky shade of pink.

Did Charlotte seriously expect them to *wear* that color?

"True or false," she said suddenly, opening her eyes. "If one outfit's success is inversely proportional to another outfit's failure, then those two outfits cancel each other out, equaling zero."

"Can you repeat that?" Laila asked, hovering a finger above her cameo pink–suited iPhone. "I lost you after 'if.' "

"She means," Kate oozed, clapping shut her frost-white iPod Touch, "does her fashion fab'ness cancel out Petra and Melissa's fashion fugly? Perhaps," she told Charlotte, dropping the glossy gadget into her signature Gucci Hysteria tote. "But at one against two, the odds aren't *exactly* in your favor."

"*Two* against two," Charlotte reminded her with a frown. "You're forgetting Janie."

"Janie," Kate snorted, rolling her eyes. "Sorry, but . . . what makes you think she'll dress any better than *they* did?"

For a moment, Charlotte's frown deepened, but then she smiled. "Oh, you know," she breathed, her chlorine eyes bright with cunning. "A little bird told me."

"I don't think birds are known for their fashion sense," Laila wisely observed, perching on Charlotte's trunk and squinting into the willow leaves.

"Trust me," she said, eyeing her friend's black lace over ivory satin Chanel headband. Her smile deepened. "She wouldn't wear a *thing* you wouldn't."

The Girl: Janie Farrish
The Getup: Black-and-white swish dress by Anna Sui (size two), dark red patent pumps by Miu Miu (size nines), and self-respect (size zero)

"So then he texts me. And he's all, Have you seen *Transformers*? And I'm like, um, you *ignore* me at my own party, *totally* get wasted, *barf* on the hood of my dad's Maybach, and you want to know if I've seen *Transformers*? Whatever! So I text him back, like, *No. Why?* And he hasn't texted me back! No, yeah, I *know*. It's been, like, an hour and a half . . ."

Janie scoured the back of the latched bathroom stall door — *anything* to distract her from Lauren Taylor's insufferably whiny cell-phone voice. Lauren had installed herself at the sinks over *five minutes ago,* and from the sound of her *fascinating* conversation, she wasn't leaving anytime soon. Janie gazed down at the toilet seat (she was such a cliché, hiding in the stall) and stifled a sigh. How she *pined* for the bathroom stalls at her old public middle school, where endlessly entertaining graffiti (the Gandhi quotes! the R.I.P. Tupacs! all the people who were apparently sluts, lesbians, or whores!) cluttered every square inch of space; but Winston stalls were made from high-tech, vandalism-repellent Kryptonite, or whatever, so she had no choice but to stare in space and just . . . listen.

"I was like, oohhh my God. You are soooo rude-uh!"

Of course, Janie reasoned, her captivity *was* self-imposed; she could always step down from the porcelain god, unlatch the stall door, and leave. And yet . . . no. No way would she have the will-power to exit the restroom without looking at the mirror, and she absolutely *hated* looking in mirrors in front of other girls, *especially* girls like Lauren, because they almost always made it into this, like, *thing.*

Was Janie the only person who found staring at herself while some other girl stared at her staring at herself seriously nerve-racking?

Okay, probably.

"It's just, like, if he doesn't have the common decency to — oh my God. Katy-Katy-Katy-Katy-I-have-to-go-he's-on-the-other-line-I know-no-I-know-I'll-call-you-back-okay-bye."

A sudden whine of door hinges wrested Janie from her stall stupor, along with a fraction of Lauren's chirpy, "Hey, baby!" The heavy door swung back, lopping the rest of her greeting with a merciful *whoosh. At last,* Janie smiled, stepping to the floor.

She was alone.

Stretching to her full five feet and ten inches, she tucked her silky brown bob behind one ear, and lifted a Tiffany & Co. shopping bag from the polished metal hook fixed to the door. She glanced inside: black leggings, vintage forest-green cardigan with faux leopard cuffs and collar, the oversize Pixies t-shirt she'd spent two hours fashioning into a rad halter dress, black-and-white-checked Vans. She glanced away, queasy with guilt. *They're just clothes,* she lectured herself. *It's not like they care whether you wear them or not.* Clattering the latch under her hand, she headed toward the wall-to-wall mirror above the automatic chrome sinks. As the maraschino Miu Miu patent pumps clacked brightly on the tile, her scorned old Vans gave a tumble, kicking the inside of the bag.

Traitor.

But it wasn't her fault! Charlotte had all but forced the glossy red shoes into her arms, accosting her at the Showroom's periphery just minutes before first bell. "You're a nine, aren't you?" she'd asked in lieu of hello. "These are eight-and-a-half's but they run small. I mean large" — Charlotte huffed — "you know what I mean. And here." She shook the Tiffany & Co. bag by its white satin rope handles. "Wear this."

"What's wrong with what I'm wearing?" Janie had ventured, daring to meet her mentor's glittering gaze. Hadn't she and Amelia Hernandez, her non-Winston-attending best friend, spent the last seven days coordinating her current ensemble? "The t-shirt halter dress is hot," Amelia had insisted. "Plus it shows creativity. *Plus* it shows you're different than those other label-dropping whores."

Since when did two pluses make a negative?

"Nothing's *wrong,*" the more popular girl assured her — but only after a painful moment's hesitation. "It's just . . . I thought for our first meeting you'd want to wear clothes they actually *sell* at Ted Pelligan. . . ." She trailed off, subjecting Janie's outfit to swift evaluation. The safety pin at her hem, the tiny moth hole at her sleeve, the dangling button at her collar: no flaw escaped her flitting, pool-green eye. *But it's vintage!* Janie wanted to cry out in protest. *As if that's any excuse,* she imagined Charlotte's reply. The popular brunette had a completely different idea of "vintage" than she did. She'd once shown up at school in a mint-condition 1960s Courrèges trapeze dress, like, "Isn't this hilarious?" As if boundary-breaking couture dresses *in perfect condition* were funny! Then again, humor came in different forms; perhaps Charlotte's was a more exclusive type? That *special* sort of humor supposedly found at Barneys, *you* know — along with "taste" and "luxury." *It's not that I've lost my sense of humor,* Janie realized, stunned; *I can't afford the right brand.*

"At least try it on?" Charlotte barged into her mind-blowing epiphany. "You can always change back into whatevs."

Hugging the bulging robin's egg blue bag to her stunted chest, Janie sighed her surrender. "Fine."

"Oh, good!" The tiny hands clapped as luxury cars continued to sail by. "But don't do it yet, okay? Wait till lunch so I can see."

Despite herself, Janie cracked a small smile. Last year, Charlotte had barely spoken to her (unless you count the occasional soul-crushing insult), and yet here she was, dressing her up like a favorite doll. Not that Janie had any illusions. She'd had favorite dolls of her own, and most of them ended up bald, dismembered, and abandoned under her bed. No doubt Charlotte was on a mission to "improve" her, to increase her value in Winston's social stock market and thereby justify their otherwise mystifying relationship. "She is so full of herself!" Amelia would later fume, incensed. But privately, Janie was grateful. More and more she'd catch girls (Farrah Frick, Bethany Snee, Nikki Pelligrini) eyeing her with a hungry, envious look — a look she recognized, having perfected it herself on Charlotte.

Of course, maybe she was overthinking? Maybe, just maybe, Charlotte *genuinely* liked her? It seemed unlikely (the girl had made Janie's ninth grade a living hell) and yet . . . stranger things were possible. She'd dated Janie's *brother*, forgodsake. True, they'd broken up, but they'd both moved on, and if Charlotte could befriend Jake, a former dorkatron who'd *cheated* on her, then what should be so bizarre about befriending Janie, a former dorkatron who . . . who *nothing*?

"Where's your brother?" Charlotte inquired lightly. Janie stared, baffled. The girl had an uncanny ability to invade her mind, but like, selectively — pocketing the one thought that interested her and casting the rest aside. Pretty crazy Jake interested her at *all*, at this point, considering their now legendary breakup and subsequent post-breakup drama. Janie smiled, relieved. Maybe they really were making an effort to be friends?

"Still in the car, I think," she recovered, gray eyes flitting to the underground parking elevator. "They're doing some kind of KROQ acoustic countdown. He was all, *if Nirvana isn't number one, I'm chaining myself to Courtney Love in protest*."

Charlotte's laughter was cut short by the growling sound of an encroaching sports car; Jules Maxwell-Langeais, Winston's imported half-English, half-French boy candy had just cruised through the black metal gate in his acid-green Ferrari. His petite girlfriend must not have realized, however, because instead of making a big show of greeting him, she kissed Janie's cheek — "Ciao!" — and bounded toward the elevator. If not for the orange-blossom fog lingering in her wake, you'd never have known she was there.

By lunch, of course, the fog had faded. But the kiss remained. With Lauren gone and Janie free to peruse her reflection, she finally noticed it: a just perceptible pink smear along her left cheekbone. She made a mental note to clean it off, but first: she turned in front of the spotless mirror. Somehow, despite Charlotte being a full foot shorter, her black-and-ivory silk dress fit perfectly, nipping her long wisp of a waist, skimming her narrow hips, and halting just below the knee. True, the dainty cap sleeves, ruffled skirt, and chaste mandarin collar were a *little* on the girlie-princess side, but the dark red four-inch stilettos more than compensated. *The dress was Snow White,* she decided.

But the shoes were poison apples.

A second whine of hinges urged her attention to the bathroom door. "Charlotte wants to know what's taking you so long," Laila informed her, a scornful eye riveted to the rounded toes of the glossy dark red pumps. The eye narrowed. "Uch," she gargled in contempt, slithering her retreat through the cracked door like an eel.

"I'll be right out," Janie called to the closing door, presenting her profile to the mirror. As she lifted a crumpled corner of paper towel to her cheek, the kiss caught the light and shimmered. *Was it a mark of protection,* she wondered, *like in* The Wizard of Oz? *Or a seal of death, like in* The Godfather. . . .

It's lipstick, she scowled, rubbing the paper roughly against her cheek. When would she stop making everything so complicated?

She exited the bathroom, her cheek throbbing pink. No longer the effect of lipstick, of course — but friction.

"Just one more thing," Charlotte advised, beckoning her forward with a backward flap of pale pink polished fingers. The signature Chanel cachalong camellia ring above her middle knuckle, along with the small hand under it, disappeared into her black satin tote, emerging later with a beautiful fabric headband.

Behind her oversize Dior sunglasses, the gorgeous brunette blinked. "Kneel?"

Janie hesitated, but did as she as she was asked: she sank to the grass and tilted her face upward. Above her, Charlotte bit her lip, clamping the hair ornament to her angled head.

"We hereby crown thee the Duchess of Doucheberry!" Theo Godfrey's thin voice warbled in the near distance. Janie thought she heard Petra's voice tell him *Shut the hell up*, but couldn't bear to turn and check. Her pale cheeks pulsed. Could Charlotte have chosen a *more* public place to officiate her totally embarrassing accessorizing ceremony?

"Magnifique!" she exclaimed, springing her fingers from Janie's temples. The Winston Willows framed the scene in feathery branches, slicing ribbons of light across the heaping plate of grapes and oozing triangle of Brie the three ballerinas called lunch. Having rejoined her friends on their cashmere Burberry blanket, Charlotte smiled, finding a grape with a polished finger and thumb. "Turn around?"

Janie turned and the green grape turned with her, snapping at the stem.

"You *do* have the legs for those shoes," Charlotte breathed, popping the grape into her mouth. Next to her, Laila paled as though she'd been pinched.

"What's *that* supposed to mean?" she squeaked, and swiftly tucked her legs under her butt, hiding what no diet, exercise, or prayer on Oprah's great earth could conquer. Her thick lower calves were the bane of her existence, her greatest weakness . . . *her Achilles cankle.* "Are you saying I *don't* have the legs for those shoes?" Laila gaped at Charlotte's insensitivity.

"And, Janie, the dress!" Charlotte tuned her out, preferring to rhapsodize. "Not everyone can pull off that ivory color."

Kate reddened, gagging on a grape.

"I'm sure these shoes would look amazing on you," Janie returned to Laila, aware of the redhead's bruised feelings, if completely mystified by them. Laila answered with a sarcastic smile.

"Oh, they *would* look amazing?"

"I can totally pull off that color!" spewed Kate, choking

down her grape and pounding the cool grass with her palm. Janie frowned with worry. Why were they taking Charlotte's comments so *personally*? Her gray eyes darted from girl to girl: Laila, clad in pink ballet slippers, and Kate, in her black camisole leotard and pink wraparound skirt. She pushed a nervous hand into her hair, forgetting the headband, which leaped from her head and flopped to the grass, coiling like a snake. A *black lace over ivory satin Chanel* snake.

Wait. Hadn't she seen that headband earlier today?

"Oh God." She whirled around to face Charlotte, her throat parched with dread. "These aren't . . . am I wearing *their* clothes?"

"What did you think?" muttered Kate as Laila sniffed beside her, eviscerating a small wedge of cheese. Between the two dance-clothed girls, Charlotte beamed.

"I explained how important this meeting was, and they *insisted* on lending them to you. Isn't that nice?" From opposite corners of the plush picnic blanket, her henchmen stiffened, and Janie broke into a sudden sweat. The black-and-ivory silk dress clung to her skin, sticking like cellophane, sealing off her pores. Just when she wondered if she really might faint, a heavenly voice echoed in her ear. *I'm dead,* she realized with relief, her gray eyes fluttering shut. *And this is the voice of an angel.*

"Whattup."

Okay, so he wasn't an angel, but with his tanned, sea salt–scrubbed skin, sun-filled, beach-sand brownish gold hair and limpid beach-glass gaze, he was the closest thing to it — well, assuming you have clichéd Renaissance notions about heaven, and looking at Evan Beverwil, just admit it: you do.

"Um . . . ew." His little sister glowered, impervious (for obvious reasons) to his brooding surfer charms. "Could you and your ghetto verbal contractions *puh-lease* take yourselves elsewhere?"

He frowned, scratching the back of his tan ankle with the toe of his navy blue Havaianas flip-flop. "Isn't 'whattup,' like, a compound word?"

"Get. Out!" Charlotte squawked, while Kate and Laila clapped their hands to their mouths, stifling their giggles. As usual, Evan had *completely* changed their personalities. It was like he'd taken the sticks out of their asses and returned them dipped in Pop Rocks. Janie turned away, repelled. Crushing on Evan Beverwil was so, like, *obvious*. Like saying, "Hawaii is beautiful." Or "French fries taste good." She, for one, resisted convention; she obsessed *outside* the box. And, yeah, *maybe* Paul Elliot Miller, the painfully hot bassist in Amelia's neopunk band Creatures of Habit, qualified as obvious. But at least he wore eyeliner, his lip ring was almost *always* infected, and he smelled — as Max, his best friend and drummer, once informed him — "like a Tequila worm, except rancid, and like, floating in a bottle of butt sweat." Janie smiled at the memory. It was weird, but liking Paul in spite of — no, *because* of — his repulsive traits, made her feel *interesting*. Like the kind of person who said, "Belarus is beautiful." Or "Deep-fried dung beetles taste good."

Of course, there was another, *simpler* reason not to lust after Evan Beverwil. He was utterly, like, *laughably* out of her league. But she preferred her complicated explanation to the more straightforward one (far better to cast yourself as a beguiling Belarusian beetle-eater than a flat-chested freak with no chance in hell).

Evan tapped the side of her wrist, snapping her from her thoughts, and trained his clear pool-green gaze on hers. "Can I talk to you for a sec?" he asked in a low voice. He tilted his head and ticked his eyes to the left, adding the unspoken, "Alone?"

"Um . . . okay." Janie shrugged, affecting a couldn't-care-less attitude. And she couldn't. The stomach spasms she attributed to gastrointestinal disorder, the light flutter in her heart to early onset angina, and as for her slightly tripped-out color-saturated vision, she blamed her mother, who had no doubt spiked her breakfast lemon yogurt with LSD. "I'll be right back," she assured Charlotte, who bobbed her delicate eyebrows and flashed Evan an evil warning look. Kate and Laila froze in disgust, two letter *W*'s etched between their eyebrows, a clue (as if Janie needed one) to what they both were thinking.

WTF.

"You totally saved me," Janie remarked once she and Evan departed the shade of the willows and were well out of earshot. She'd meant to sound offhand and ironic, and might have succeeded if Joaquin Whitman hadn't picked up his guitar and floated a quiet, tender melody across the lawn. Melancholy guitar music has a way of making anything you say sound nauseatingly sincere.

You totally saved me. "I mean" — she raised her voice, attempting to drown out the Lifetime soundtrack — "Laila and Kate pretty much want me dead right now."

"Oh yeah?" Evan appeared to think deeply on the subject. "Why?"

"I don't know," she replied. *What if she explained and he took their side?* "Where are we going?"

"The Brat." He began walking.

Janie nodded. And then she smiled. That she'd just *known* what "the Brat" *meant*; it seemed significant somehow. Sliding her eyes to the left, she pondered Evan's serious profile: the sandy brown eyebrows, the long blond-tipped lashes, the barely sunburned bridge of his nose, the soft dent in his rose-wax lower lip. They'd only had five or six conversations, each of them more inept than the last, and yet — actual information *must* have been exchanged. How else would she know the pet name for his Porsche? Or that he had nightmares about the elephant statues at the La Brea Tar Pits? And his ongoing obsession with Bob Seger, or the very strange fact that he'd read *Are You There God? It's Me, Margaret*? Weren't these the kind of dorky details dudes like Evan Beverwil kept close to the vest? The kind of details you'd never guess unless, well . . . you *knew* them?

"What?" He paused at the gleaming door of his fire engine red Porsche 911 convertible. Janie blanched, suddenly aware that she'd been staring.

"Oh," she shook her head quickly. "Nothing."

Pushing some air from between his lips, Evan bobbed his eyebrows — *whatever* — and grabbed the door handle. Planting one navy blue flip-flop on the ground, he slid into the black leather–upholstered driver's seat, craned sideways, and popped open the glove compartment. His faded moss green Pintail t-shirt strained across his broad back, inched above the waistline of his navy-silver board shorts, and revealed a tantalizing stretch of taut, tanned torso. Then the glove compartment clapped shut, and the t-shirt closed down like a curtain.

"Here," he gestured, getting out of the car. A flimsy Utrecht Art Supplies bag dangled under his hand. He presented it to her, scratching the back of his neck.

"What is this?" Janie frowned with mock suspicion. Plastic rustled around her wrist as she hesitatingly reached inside, removing a cellophane-sealed tin box. "Oh . . . ," she breathed. It was a Prismacolor Premier colored pencil set, 132 pencils, the largest set available. Of course, at $190-something, she'd had to restrict herself to the more modestly priced twelve-pencil set, a familiar array of colors like crimson red, grass green, lemon yellow, black, and white. But here in her hands, so much more: Copenhagen blue, celadon green, dahlia purple, Spanish orange. Colors so beautiful they made her heart ache. *Why is he giving this to me?* she wondered. And then, inanely, an answer:

He likes me?

"So," his boyish voice echoed behind her dreamlike thoughts. "I was thinking, like, maybe you could help me design something?"

Briskly, Janie glanced up, attempting to shake off her daze. "Design . . . what?"

"A *tattoo*," he half smiled, like he'd had to repeat himself. "I'm turning eighteen in a couple months, and like, I want something custom-drawn. Look," he added, all business, "it's not like I wouldn't *pay* you."

"Oh," she replied, allowing the mists to part. Returning the pencil set to the bag, she happened to glimpse her reflection in his curved, tinted sports car window. Her mutant face smeared across the glass, expanding on one side like a half-wet sponge. That she'd actually allowed herself to think he *liked* her!

It was so impossibly pathetic.

"You know what, I'm sure you're busy, so don't worry about —"

"No, no!" she stopped him, whipping away from the car window. "I'll do it, I mean" — attempting to mask her sponge face behind her hands, she glanced up — "I'd like to."

"Oh," he nodded slowly. "Cool."

The bell rang, signaling the end of lunch. All around them, car doors unlocked, hiccuping mechanical chirps, and kids began to mosey to their cars, glugging the dregs of their bottled Cokes and organic Kombucha teas. Janie gave Evan a nervous smile, *I should go,* and turned to leave.

"I meant to ask you," he stopped her. She turned around again, more alert than ever to the surrounding rabble — the wheezing hydraulics, the car trunk *kuh-klunks,* the shrieking laughter.

"Weren't you wearing something different before?"

"Oh," she flushed. Would he realize her clothes belonged to Charlotte's friends? Would he think she stole them from a coat check, Lindsay Lohan–style? "Um, yeah," she confessed miserably.

"I thought so," he pursed his lips, upwardly tilting his chin. "I was going to tell you, like, cool shoes. But then you changed, so . . ."

She frowned, hugging the plastic bag to her chest. It made a sound like dead leaves.

"*Not* that what you're wearing now *isn't* cool," he quickly backtracked. "But . . ."

"But . . . ?" she prompted, squeezing out a terrible laugh. She could only imagine his response: but you're too tall for high heels. But you're too tomboyish for dresses. But you're too sponge-faced to live.

But what?

"Nothing, it's just" — his chlorine green eyes locked into middle distance, the pupils furling into small points — "it's just what you were wearing before was more, like, *you*. You know?"

Janie's heart rose in her throat. She swallowed, daring to meet his half-moon-shaped pool green eyes. She'd never heard "you" said in quite that way. Like "you" was something good. Something *complimentary*, even.

Like "you" was something she didn't need to change.

The Miu Miu's

The Me Me's

vs.

Janie Farrist

The Girl: Miss Paletsky
The Getup: Beige pleated linen-blend pants, white polyester chiffon wraparound blouse, nude nylon trouser socks, and white strappy sandals, all from Marshalls. Watermelon-shaped shoulder purse from Russian street market

"Do you see the *earrings* on that one?" gasped Ms. DeWitt, pant-suited fossil of Winston's Earth and Sciences Department and proud proprietress of the wondrously wide and fantastically flat posterior Winston students had nicknamed *the Tundra*. Ms. DeWitt ritualistically scanned the babbling horde on the brushed-concrete Assembly Hall floor, picking one face out of hundreds for critique. "They're enormous," she continued, clucking under her dinosaur breath. "I'm surprised she can hold her *head* up, poor thing!"

Miss Paletsky, the young Russian Director of Special Studies, blinked behind her octagon-shaped LensCrafters, noting the "poor thing" in question. The flaxen-haired eighth-grader's fist-size golden bamboo hoops swayed below her ears and bumped against her canary yellow cardigan-clad shoulders, causing the surrounding girls to collectively gasp in . . . dismay? *No* — she revised her judgment, regarding their ecstatic expressions — *admiration*. During the past month, Nikki Pellegrini's social standing had swung dramatically — she was popular one minute, persecuted the next — for reasons no teacher could fathom. Now, it seemed, she was popular again — and Miss Paletsky surmised it had something to do with Poseur. Nikki had just been recruited as their new intern, replacing a devastated Venice Whitney-Wang. (Upon her dismissal, Venice had flailed into her office wailing like a war widow; evidently, Poseur was *the* class to be in, and (even as she folded the sobbing girl into her arms) Miss Paletsky had to admit — she was the teensiest bit proud. After all, without her urging and foresight? It would have never existed.)

"Did you see Charlotte Beverwil?" Mrs. Dang worried aloud, interrupting the younger teacher's rumination. Despite the screaming volume, the geometry instructor lowered her voice to a whisper. "Those *shoes*, I mean . . . what if the poor dear falls?"

Miss Paletsky shifted her focus to the west wall, the designated domain of Charlotte Beverwil and her venerated überwealthy indie set: pouty girls in black eyeliner, angled bangs, and knotted silk scarves, bored boys in rumpled shirts, stovepipe pants, and tousled pompadours. *The Bardots and Belmondos of Beverly Hills,* she mused, referring, of course, to the icons of the French New Wave. Kate Joliet, Laila Pikser, Bronwyn Spencer, Tim Beckerman, Luke Christie, Emma Raub, Adelaide Dallas, Jules Maxwell-Langeais, and (recently added to their ranks and not quite blending in) twin scholarshipniks Janie and Jake Farrish; all sat on the floor, backs against the brick wall, except, of course, the stunning chlorine-eyed brunette, who'd remained standing, one controversial shoe kicked up behind her — an imperious flamingo among a flock of pigeons.

"I'm sure *one* of those shoes costs a *month's* salary," sighed the incredulous Mrs. Dang, shaking her head. *Imagine.*

"Oh, at *least*." The Tundra narrowed her eyes and quaked.

"Stop," lisped Señor Smith. The ginger-haired, baby-faced Spanish instructor clutched his heart, darted his pale eyes between them. He affected a scandalized expression. "You people make *that* much?"

"All right, people!" Glen Morrison, the self-elected moderator of Winston Prep's biweekly Town Meeting danced along the north wall and halted their banter, clapping his hands. "Let's get this party started!" Like a well-trained mime troupe, the collected faculty snapped into character and dispersed through the boisterous crowd. Every three seconds, one stopped to loom above a cheerfully unaware chatterer, until, sensing a creeping chill, the offender glanced up and immediately withered into silence. Inevitably, the faculty reconvened at the Back Wall, aka "Stonehedge," a ruined country of cackling, semicollapsed potheads who could not, no matter how urgently and repeatedly they were hushed, shut the hell up. Trudging into this unruly mass, teachers often became mired, unable to emerge until Town Meeting was dismissed. They just stood there, trapped, like cows in a swamp.

"Theo, Christina, Petra!" bellowed the bullnecked Coach Hollander, squeezing his fists until his '84 garnet class ring just about popped. "I mean it!" he sputtered as Joaquin Whitman stuffed his iPod headphones into his nose and emphatically sneezed them onto Theo's shoulder. *"Joaquin!"*

"So, I have a very exciting announcement to make," continued Glen. Once the volume decreased to his satisfaction, he gripped the podium and turned around. "Regarding one of our newest teachers." Sitting on one of the metal folding chairs reserved for faculty along the North Wall, Miss Paletsky smiled blandly, then froze, realizing herself to be the subject of Glen's twinkly-eyed attention. He extended his left arm, sleeved in wide-grooved, olive-brown corduroy, and beckoned her forward. "Miss Paletsky?"

Squeezing a sheath of papers to her chest, she nervously approached, aided by the encouraging, if sporadic, claps from the student body. What could he possibly want with her? Reaching the podium, she tipped into a tiny bow, spilling her octagon-shaped LensCrafters down her nose. As she fumbled to correct them, Glen dropped his hand on her shoulder, disarranging her shoulder pad.

His smile was menacingly gentle.

"Because she's *too shy* to tell you herself," he reported, offering the crowd a teasing wink, "I'm just going to have to announce the happy news for her." The young Russian teacher's face paled — it was only too clear what Glen was up to — and she tried to shake her head. "Ladies and gentlemen," he cried. She closed her eyes, clutching her papers like a life raft. "Miss Paletsky's engaged!"

Predictably, all three hundred students erupted into deafening, shrieking applause. Miss Paletsky struggled to smile. She couldn't imagine they cared — not *really*. More like they needed an excuse to scream and Glen gave them one (they'd expressed similar mania when he'd announced the availability of raisin-free cinnamon bagels). Under different circumstances, of course, she might have enjoyed their overly enthusiastic outburst, but circumstances being what they were, she could only stand there and endure. *If only you knew,* she mentally addressed them, struggling to smile. *You're rejoicing the end of all ch'appiness. You're cheering the death of my ch'eart!*

Miss Paletsky had finally agreed to marry Yuri Grigorovich, the stocky, stained-wife-beater-wearing owner of the Copy & Print store on Fairfax, not for love — *ch'a!* — but for green card. Her worker's visa was about to expire, and unless she took action, it was (in the words of her fetid fiancé) "back to Russia like a dog." She had deliberated her answer as long as possible, fretting in her doll-size bungalow apartment, staring through her one window at the avocado trees on North Vista Street. She may loathe Yuri, but at least she trusted him — and how could she go back to Moscow? It was a city of ghosts: her parents, grandparents, temperamental, laughing Masha, and Otar — beautiful Otar in his Kobe Bryant jersey! All of them dead. And then, the terrible night she was robbed at gunpoint walking home from the conservatory — she'd been practicing until two a.m., transported, as usual, by Beethoven. That winter had been breathtakingly cold. At home, with only a thin blanket for warmth, she slept under a pile of laundry, clean and dirty mixed together. Her landlady gave her a space heater, but she never used it — the wiring was faulty, and there were fires.

That, she would never forget.

Compared to such things, what was it to marry Yuri? Nothing, and yet . . .

One night, walking home after a particularly grueling commute on the L.A. Metro bus, she'd misread *N. Vista* as *No Visa*. Twilight had obscured her eyesight, the street sign was old and faded, she was dead tired: all good excuses, all wrong. *It was either to make decision,* she realized, lying awake at night. *Or slowly to go mad.*

In the end, a man named Christopher Duane Moon made up her mind. He breezed into her office last month, smiled, and the whole world . . . opened up. Just like that, she could breathe again. She felt *free*. But feelings are feelings, reality is reality. *My fiancée,* he'd said, casual as anything — and the world squeezed tighter than ever before. He was *engaged*.

Of course he was.

She moved into the smallest and beigest of Yuri's three bedrooms — the "Mankiev room," named after Russian wrestler and Olympic gold-medalist Nazyr Mankiev, whose imposing five-by-six-foot poster, lovingly hung on the windowless east wall, constituted the room's sole decoration. Upon her arrival, her pungent prince presented her with a pair of bride and groom stuffed bears, two polished brass keys, and an engagement band of roughly the same color. The bears she placed on her Ikea Billy bookcase alongside the framed photograph of her grandparents, a potted philodendron, her lock-and-key diary, and a small plaster bust of Beethoven. With the exception of her old Emerson upright piano, which she'd had to leave in the living room opposite Yuri's gigantic plasma screen TV, these meager tokens served as the only evidence of her former existence. She'd sold her pale green flower dishes, donated her birch-wood futon, and bought a new toothbrush that — for the first time ever — wasn't blue, but yellow. Her yellow toothbrush said: *I am starting a new life.*

Her yellow toothbrush said: *I am dead.*

The town meeting applause had yet to die down, and so Lena Paletsky hid her pale face behind her hands, masking her despair as modesty. Through the bright slats of her fingers she witnessed Charlotte Beverwil spring to her heels, clapping daintily, and Janie Farrish follow suit, bouncing on her toes. Nikki Pellegrini hammered her knees — earrings aquiver — and a dancing Petra Greene floated her arms into the air, twirling like a wind sprite. *Such exuberance!* But (she couldn't help but wonder) where was the most exuberant girl of all? Where was the daughter of the man who so casually opened and closed the world?

Melissa Moon remained seated, nudged against the East Wall,

her defined chin planted firmly on her knees. A soft, resigned sadness darkened her lovely face, and recognizing it, the Russian teacher lowered her hands from her face.

They locked eyes and almost smiled.

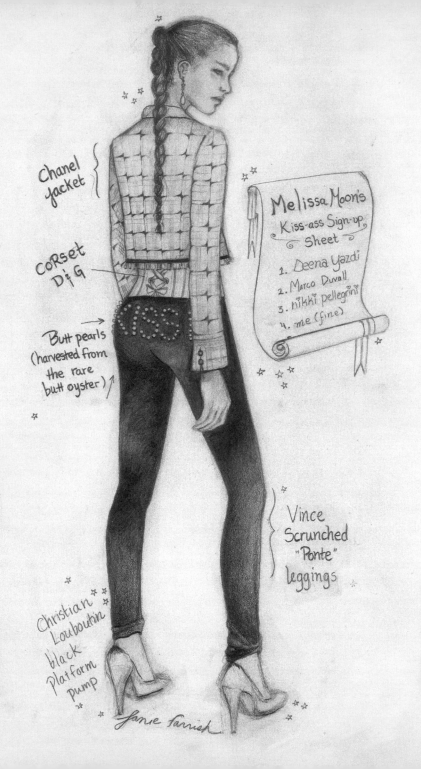

Chanel
jacket

CORSET
D & G

Butt pearls
(harvested from
the rare
butt oyster)

Melissa Moon's
Kiss-ass Sign-up
Sheet
1. Deena Yazdi
2. Marco Duvall
3. nikki pellegrini
4. me (fine)

Vince
Scrunched
"Ponte"
leggings

Christian
Louboutin
black
Platform
pump

Janie Farrish

The Guy: Jake Farrish
The Getup: Navy blue Dickies, gray low-top Converse All-Stars, black-and-white-checked vintage button-down, dark green American Apparel hoodie

"Girl, I'll be there in a *second*." Marco Duvall tore his focus from his pickup half-court game just long enough to catch his girlfriend's indignant you-cannot-be-serious eye. At times like this he really resented the court's center Showroom placement. *Whatever,* he grimaced, glancing away. Could she *not* see Farrish had the ball palmed (for a skinny dude, hands were *big*), and ticktocked above that crazy rooster hairdo of his? Did she seriously want him to miss this opportunity?

"Yo!" Marco shouldered his way through the sweat-stained, sneaker-squeaking dude mass, envisioning himself a pinnacle of masculine prowess. Jake spotted him, readied the ball, and —

"No, no, please!" A formal transatlantic male voice pierced through the grunting cacophony. Jules Maxwell-Langeais, all GQ'ed out in charcoal chinos, a body-hugging white Henley, and powder blue boaters, raised a deeply tanned arm. "I yam open!" he called, squinting like a man saluting from his yacht.

Marco's eyes bulged in their sockets. Had he *not* made himself clear?

"YO!!!"

But Jake had made a promise and was, for the time being, a

dude of his word — especially where Charlotte was concerned. She'd come to see him that morning, braving the dismal descent underground, a surprise move in two respects: 1) Charlotte was strictly upper level, a purebred "Showroom pony," and underground parking was, literally and figuratively, beneath her, and 2) they'd just emerged from a pretty epic breakup. Yes, at his twin sister's insistence, they'd agreed to cut out the dramatics, but without dramatics, what had they been left with? "Hey." "Hey." "So . . ." "How was your weekend?" "Oh. Um. It was good. Yours?" "Good! I DustBustered my car."

Something about saying "DustBustered" to your ex-girlfriend. It seriously just . . . cripples the will.

Rather than risk running into her again, Jake had decided to hole up in underground parking. *You* know. Bruce Wayne–style. Imagine his surprise when, after four minutes of perfect solitude, the black Volvo door cracked open and there she was, slipping into the front seat, all smiles, sweet perfume, and things to say. Imagine his surprise when he just *said things back*. Like, they'd both just decided, at the exact same time, *not* to be awkward.

That is, until she brought *him* up.

"Jules told me you guys are playing basketball later?" Charlotte propped her death heel on the duct-taped dash. "You know, it's really important to him that he improve his game."

"Oh yeah?" Jake replied, still staring at her foot. The fact that Jules "told" her stuff — the fact that she *listened* — it was all so horribly graphic. Seriously, he could handle the fact that they were dating. But that they *talked* to each other? That they "shared"? He frowned. *Some of this shit she should keep to herself.*

"So," she pressed on. "Why don't you guys pass him the ball?"

"What?" Jake pushed out an uneasy laugh, crumpling his forehead. "We . . . pass him the ball." *When they felt like throwing the game.*

"Jake," she admonished him, folding her arms across her chest, and her silk skirt shifted, sliding a good two inches up her thigh. *It's fun to lose,* Kurt Cobain buzzed inside the shitty speakers, drowning in subterranean static. *And to-oo pretend . . .*

"It isn't nice," she sighed. "Just because he's my boyfriend, you . . ."

Boyfriend?!!

"Fine!" he blurted, punching the radio off. "I'll tell the guys to pass him the ball . . . I mean, more than we have been. Which is a lot. Relatively."

"Good!" Charlotte breathed. "Then I agree to study for Ms. McGovern's vocab quiz with you."

Jake lifted an eyebrow and slid his dark brown eyes sideways. They hadn't discussed studying together. So why was she was smiling at him like they'd had a long-standing plan?

"Monday night?" she chimed, as if to remind him.

"I don't know." He glanced away and frowned, picking some duct tape on the dash. He was all for being friends, but *studying* together? For *vocab*? Was he seriously supposed to *not* touch her as she sat there oh-so-enticingly asking him to define obfuscate? Pernicious? *Disseminate?*

"Come on, Jake." Charlotte sounded almost plaintive. "I made flash cards."

"Oh man, *flash cards*." He looked up and sighed, regarding the manipulative and yet painfully adorable baby-in-a-poopy-diaper expression on her face. *"Okay,"* he laughed, and pushed her shoulder, making it go away. "We'll study."

And so he jolted back to the present, just seven hours after their chum-fest, passing the ball to his rival, hurling it with all his might. Marco Duvall groaned with despair as the orange sphere arced through the air, out of his capable grasp, and into Jules's outstretched hands. The ponytailed exchange student gripped the ball, facing him with childlike triumph.

"Shoot the ball!" Marco yelled in strangled disbelief.

But it was too late. Leon Gorlach roared in like an uncensored episode of National Geographic, swiping the ball into his possession and carrying it off like a good-as-dead baby hippo. Twisting high into the air, the wiry ninth-grader cranked his arm back, tongue lolling, and tore that hoop a new hoop-hole.

"Ee-YEAH, baybee!!!" He pounded the pavement, swung his clenched, raw-knuckled fist, and thumped his pigeon chest. *"Posterized."*

"He is good, no?" Jules sidled up to Jake, addressing him in a confidential tone.

"Yeah." Jake squinted through his dripping dark brown hair.

Seemed Gorlach had moved on from thumping his chest to sniffing his armpits. "Poetry in motion."

"I would not go so far as that!" Jules laughed, missing Jake's sarcasm by about a mile and a half. Marco observed their interaction under a disapproving yet sympathetic brow. He knew what Farrish was thinking: *So my girlfriend dumped me. Did she have to move on to this clown?* Marco made a mental note to educate his scrawny ass: "Listen," he'd say — maybe put his hand on his shoulder or some shit like that — "smokin' hot girls be hookin' up with clowns since the *dawn of time*. Just the way it *is*. Have it hardwired into their smokin' hot *DNA*."

Well, except for *his* girlfriend, of course.

"Marco, do not *even* touch me!" Melissa shrieked as he approached her with wide-open arms, ready to reel her into a sweaty-ass bear hug. Her chicken-head friends got all quiet, gathering around the platinum Lexus convertible, like, *Oh no you didn't.* "I told you," Melissa reminded him, ducking behind her annoying friend Deena. "You play b-ball and you forfeit all rights to touch me."

"Thought maybe you'd change your mind," he grinned, lifting his *I'm a Rock Star in Jamaica* t-shirt to wipe his face. ('Cause, yeah. *Someone* brought the six-pack to the barbecue.) His white-hot girlfriend grimaced, yanking his shirt down.

"Change my mind?" Her black eyes snapped. "I have the most important meeting of my *life* in less than an hour."

Looking wounded, he smoothed his mauled t-shirt over his unappreciated abs. "So?"

"Deena." Melissa fluttered her dark eyes shut, spanking the air. "Will you explain this to him?"

"Boy," her horse-faced best friend began, fanning her tiny, pinched nose with her French-manicured hand. "You think she want to show up at Ted Pelligan with your *man*-stink all over her?"

"Whoa, whoa, Dino, hold up." Marco forked a hand into his springing brown curls, looking puzzled. "You mean to say you can *smell* outta that nose job?"

"For the last time!" Deena squawked, flushing an angry shade of puce while her traitor friends hid their smiles. "I had a *deviated septum*. Without necessary surgical intervention, I could have *died*, Marco!"

Just as a crowd began to gather, a nasal beeping filled the air, grinding the performance to a sudden halt. A dozen girls turned to face their intruder, their exfoliated foreheads in various stages of rumpled disapproval.

"So sorry to interrupt your *turf* wars," Charlotte Beverwil chimed, fluttering a wave from the depths of her lumbering vintage Jag. Janie Farrish sat half-slumped in the driver's seat, her bobbed light-brown hair delicately mussed, and a pretty fair imitation of Charlotte's *ennui* smacked across her face. "Just wanted to bid y'all adieu," Charlotte called, focusing in on Melissa. "That's French, by the way. For *outie*."

In a burst of panic, Melissa scampered to the side of the vehicle. No *way* was she letting Charlotte and her paraffin-pampered paws get to Ted Pelligan first. She could just *see* it: the two of them, chillin' in the corner office, chuckling over some private joke. How *dare* they have a private joke? She hadn't even *introduced* herself yet!

"No!" She gripped the lip of the window, forcing Charlotte to a sudden brake.

"What do you mean, *no*?" Her raven head jerked forward.

"We have to wait for Petra," Melissa warned, gripping the window tighter.

"Um, no." Charlotte frowned, cranking the volume on her longtime obsesh: Beirut. "Petra's *your* car, remember?"

"Well, we need to caravan," she insisted, raising her voice above what sounded like dueling accordions. "What if one of us gets lost?"

Charlotte arched an icy cool eyebrow. Melissa knew as well as she did — one just didn't "get lost" on the way to Ted Pelligan. Winston girls were like newly hatched baby turtles, and Ted Pelligan? *Was the sea.* Were baby turtles afraid of getting lost? Did baby turtles quote-unquote *caravan*?

No. The baby turtles just *knew*.

Charlotte narrowed her glittering green eyes in suspicion. Melissa wanted to get to Ted Pelligan first. The question was *pourquoi*? So she could convince him *butt* pearls were the wave of the future?

Without another moment's hesitation, she sank her heel to the gas.

"No, you did *not!*" Melissa called after her screeching wheels, flapping her impossibly toned arms.

"Oh yes, she did," a throaty voice piped up behind her. Melissa whirled around. *Well,* she scowled. *If it isn't my belated bohemian friend.*

"Get in the car," she barked, snapping her fingers in the direction of the gleaming Lexus.

"Relax, El Snapitan," Petra quipped, raising her blue-ink-stained hands in surrender. Melissa balled up her fists, pulsing like a nuclear flash.

"Now!"

Miss Dillydally darted toward the car.

Petra Greene is Business Casual...

"I still don't understand," Charlotte sighed, flattening her ballerina back against her butter-tan leather seat. The winding canyon was behind them now, and the Jaguar coasted onto a wide and smoothly paved avenue bordered by majestic sun-filled pines. For the last five minutes, Janie had been staring out the window, dreaming up surfer tattoos: winding seaweed vines, and shark teeth, electric eels, and mermaids. At the sound of Charlotte's voice they blew away like dust.

"What?" she turned from the window, blinking. *Please, God. Let her* not *have just read my mind*. Seriously, weren't telepathic powers supposed to be limited to, like, kooky great-aunts and glittering vampires? The former always had your best interests at heart. And the latter only threatened to suck your blood — not your very last drop of dignity.

"Nothing." The witch at the wheel eyed her up and down. "It's just . . . I liked the other outfit better, that's all."

"Yeah." Janie gazed at her leopard-print cardigan cuffs, smoothing the faux fur over her wrists. "I just . . . this outfit just feels more *me*, or something."

With a delicate bob of her eyebrows, Charlotte adjusted her pearl gray Hermès driver's glove. For the life of her she would never understand girls who thought *comfort* was, like, a legitimate style choice. When would they realize "me" marked the halfway point to *mess*?

She resolved to change the subject.

"So, what did my *brother* say to you?"

"Oh," Janie blushed. "Nothing, he — he wanted to know if I could design him a tattoo."

"Are you kidding me?" Charlotte rolled her eyes. "You're not going to, are you?"

Janie chewed her thumbnail.

"Janie!" she spanked the wheel in disbelief. "Don't waste your talent on such folderol. Your time is precious!"

"It shouldn't take that long." She shrugged, smiling into her lap. That Charlotte thought she was talented! That she'd deigned to say so!

"Uchh . . ." The driver regarded her pleased profile with suspicion. "Do you have a crush on my brother?"

"What?" Janie wheezed out a laugh and blushed. "Um, *no*."

"Oh, I'm sorry," Charlotte fluttered her eyelashes, not bothering to hide her smile. "I didn't mean to make you . . . *uncomfortable*."

"I'm *not*," Janie gaped, tucking her bob behind her ear, "*uncomfortable*. It's just . . . I mean . . . we're just . . ."

"Friends?" offered the pretty brunette, flipping the turn signal to an appallingly boner-like angle. Janie glanced away.

"Yeah," she exhaled.

"Too bad I don't believe in male-female friendships," Charlotte rejoined, pleased by her trap's success. She slid Janie a knowing look. "Call me *old-fashioned*, but someone's *always* hiding an attraction."

Janie narrowed her eyes. Of all the things she'd love to call Charlotte right now, "old-fashioned" was so *not* one of them. And then something occurred to her.

"What about you and Jake?"

The turn signal clicked, sproinging downward, and Charlotte screwed up her face, shifting in her seat. "What *about* me and Jake?"

"If there's no such thing as —"

"Jules and I are *really serious*," she cut her off, cranking the polished wood wheel.

"I know," Janie began.

"*No,*" Charlotte snapped before she could continue. "You don't."

Janie faced the window and flinched, fighting off the sting. Charlotte was right, of course. Pretty much the closest Janie had come to a serious relationship was back in fourth grade, when Michael McFadden handed her a green M&M and said, "The green ones make you horny." Since then, it had all been downhill. *Still,* she thought, watching the neon signs on Sunset Boulevard flash dimly in the daylight. That Charlotte just *said* so with such absolute *authority*. Like Janie's utter lack of experience was just, like, *splattered* all over her face.

It pissed her off.

"I know more than you think," she informed her condescending driver, still glaring out the window. "It's not like I've never had a boyfriend."

Charlotte exhaled quickly through her nostrils and curved the corner of her mouth into a smile. "Really."

Janie moistened her slightly chapped lips. She hadn't *wanted* to embellish her lie, but Charlotte's rage-inducing response all but forced her at gunpoint. "You know Creatures of Habit?"

"Sounds familiar," she replied slowly. Janie smiled. Her best friend Amelia had a pet peeve with people who said "sounds familiar." *It's only, like, the deadest giveaway they have no idea what you're talking about,* she'd scoff, dripping with contempt.

"Oh, they're just this band," Janie continued in her best I-can't-believe-you-haven't-heard-of-them tone. "Anyway" — leaning forward in her seat, she gripped the glove compartment and smiled — "he's the bassist."

"Oh, *really*?" Charlotte waited out the light on Sunset and Hillcrest, pale fingers toying with the clustered cabbage ruffles at her throat. "What's this bassist's name?"

Janie's seat belt tightened against her chest. Something about saying his name out loud: it made her nervous. Her instinct was to backpedal, maybe make up a name — but what if Charlotte Googled Creatures of Habit? She fretted, examining Charlotte's haughty profile.

She kind of seemed like a closet compulsive Googler.

"Paul," Janie croaked, and pulled the seat belt toward her lap. "I mean, he's not, like, my *boyfriend* boyfriend. He's more like . . . you know." She swallowed. "We're kind of off and on."

Charlotte drummed her clear polished fingernails against the wheel. Was it just her, or was Janie making "off and on" sound way more appealing than "serious"? With all those breathy little pauses and glazed faraway looks. Uch! *She totally was.* But off-and-on relationships *aren't* appealing, Charlotte reminded herself. Off-and-on relationships lead on to heartbreak! *And passion,* countered the beret-wearing devil on her shoulder. *All of your favorite couples.* Jean-Paul Sartre and Simone de Beauvoir. Napoléon and Josephine. Elizabeth Taylor and Richard Burton. *Miss Piggy and Kermit?*

Admit it, he cackled. *You miss that feeling.*

"Hey, sexy!" A shrill voice called from a neighboring lane, and Charlotte gave a start, glancing left. *"Mm!"* Petra leered over the passenger side of Melissa's gleaming platinum Lexus convertible, purple shades glinting in the sun, hair flying all over the place. "You ladies are looking *fine.*"

"Get a grip, creep," Charlotte deadpanned, just as the light flicked green. She barely had time to react before Melissa slammed on the gas, peeling off with an impressive squeal. *"Merde!"* she cried, fumbling for the pedal while Janie clutched the sides of her buttery leather seat. Ahead of them — so far ahead! — Madame Pearlbutt lifted her tan arm in mocking salute, bright bangles flashing on her wrist. Charlotte swallowed a hard lump of pride, daring to ask a question she never, in a *billion* lifetimes, thought she'd ask.

Why can't I be more like Melissa?

The only man on *her* mind was Ted Pelligan.

The Gent: Ted Pelligan
The Getup: Lime green seersucker suit and white shirt by Paul Smith, lavender sunshine medallion silk tie by Ermenegilda Zegna, traditional two-tone wing tips by Salvatore Ferragamo, silver silicone Men's Elite Gardening Gloves by Bionic Gloves

In Theodore Pluto Pelligan the IV's humble point of view, luxury retailers existed not merely to *clothe* souls, but to *alter* them. Which was to say, even if a customer entered his store and left buying *nothing*, he or she should still feel ineluctably *changed*. A store's *ambience* — the lighting (tasteful), the prices (wasteful), the staff (unsmiling), the music (beguiling), the scent (a bouquet-stuffed *boudoir*), the attitude (make *luxury*, not war) — was as important, if not *more* important, than the objects it sold. He compared the experience to his own — many years ago, now — at Harvard; he was there for ten glorious minutes, left with *nothing* (save a Polaroid of Mother on the steps of Widener Library), and yet, he'd been forever *transformed*. The true worth of Harvard, he decided, was rooted in *ambience* — not the paltry *degree* it peddled.

So formative was his experience, he designed his flagship Melrose store with the university in mind: an impressive building, bordered by pathways of venerable red brick, and absolutely *covered* — from the lip of the sidewalk to the tip of the two-story roof — in *gorgeous* green ivy. Of course, in places his leafy creepers had to be (ah! his favorite word) *pruned*; that is, cleared away to better showcase the window displays, *not to mention* his *name*, which appeared on the wall in alternating blue and crimson letters. He hoped Ted Pelligan, like Harvard, would one day become synonymous with "crème de la crème."

And it had.

HARVARD + TED PELLIGAN:
A COMPARATIVE ANALYSIS

Common Peasant: Where did you go to college?

Someone Fabulous, Like You: In Cambridge.

Peasant: Where in Cambridge?

You: Oh, um . . . Harvard.

Peasant: Really? Wow. Harvard. Well, tra-la-la, Little Miss Fancy-Pants!

You (lying): It's not really like that.

Common Peasant: Omigod! Where did you get that top?

Someone Fabulous, Like You: On Melrose.

Peasant: Where on Melrose?

You: Oh, um . . . Ted Pelligan.

Peasant: Really? Wow. Ted Pelligan. Well, tra-la-la, Little Miss Fancy-Pants!

You (lying): They were having a sale.

But the two institutions' affinity wasn't meant to last. In the 1980s, when Harvard *removed* their ivy due to *apparent* wall deterioration and steep labor costs, it stung, to be quite frank, like a spank in the face. Beside himself with grief, *racked* by betrayal, Ted did what any self-avenging citizen would do: angrily, he wrote them a letter.

```
Dear Harvard,
I, for one, valeu my ivy, and as for
stepe labre costs, I trimm
the stuff myself.
                    Disgustidly,
                    T.P.¹
```

"Teddy?" His assistant, Gideon Peck, who spoke in the low, respectful tone of a funeral director even when ordering pizza, pushed open the polished wood door, ducking his solemn young face into the large, stately office. Discovering the brass-studded burgundy leather wing chair empty, he heaved his hangdog gaze to the opposite side of the vast room. As expected, his silver-haired superior crouched catlike by one of four dormer windows, an enormous pair of steel shears in hand. A tiny green tendril of ivy, having stealthily unfurled in the dead of night, peered through the open window, quivering in the breeze.

"Just look at it, Giddy," he murmured in his unplaceable

---

¹ Like fellow geniuses Leonardo da Vinci, Thomas Edison, and Cher, Ted Pelligan was gifted with dyslexia.

accent, like a 1930s film star's, and squinted behind his rimless rectangular glasses. *"Brazen as a Peeping Tom."*

The assistant stepped into the room. "Sir . . ."

"Just a moment." Mr. Pelligan hushed him, quietly crept forward, and wet his pale lips with the tip of his tongue. The shears flashed — *snippity-snip!* Exhaling, he retreated a step, stooped, and pinched the tender green sprig between his fingers. As he marched it toward his desk, Gideon bowed his head, clasping his hands.

"His green seraglio has its eunuchs too," Mr. Pelligan intoned, beautifully trilling his *r*'s. His silver-gloved fingers parted, and the sprig fell soundlessly into a waiting brass bin. *"Lest any tyrant him outdo."*

A moment of silence.

"Yes?" He turned suddenly, sweeping his rimless eyewear from behind his smallish pink ears and fluttering his silver lashes. "What is it?"

"Your four o'clock, sir." Gently, Gideon wrested the shears from his superior's small, garden-gloved hand and carried them to the antique maple highboy behind the desk, cleaning the blade with a brisk motion across his sleeve. "The young ladies of Poseur," he droned, taking care with his pronunciation as he slid open the second-to-top maple drawer.

"Ah!" his superior exclaimed, yanking the squared fingertips of his garden gloves one by one. "My sweet damsels in design. My most *darling* of discoveries. *Allez!*" He freed his hand and wiggled his plump, bejeweled fingers. "Send them in."

Gideon cracked a small smile. Teddy loved nothing more than to hatch new talent, and he always *could* spot a good egg. His prodigies included Chloë Sevigny, Vikki Beckham, Stella McCartney, and, of course, Miss Ashley and Miss Mary-Kate. "When I found them they were just a couple of impossibly thin, identically pouted billionaires with all their Tiffany hearts could desire!" he was fond of recounting. "But they had *pluck*, Giddy, and I could tell . . . these girls were *going* places. I took them under my wing. I said, *'I know what you're going through*. The world seems a warm, friendly place . . . you feel so happy it's a damn *miracle* you make it out of bed! *But,* my lovelies, you have *got* to move *on.*' 'How?' they asked. Can you *imagine*? The darlings! 'I know it's easier *done* than *said,'* I told them, *'but . . . why not start a fashion line?'* The *looks* on their faces, Giddy. Like I'd just opened a door into a world of privilege *exactly* like the one they were already in!"

The Olsen girls went on to create two industry-respected luxury labels, The Row and Elizabeth & James, and then flew the nest, making a permanent home of New York. The move was only natural — it was New York, after all, not its yoga-panted West Coast cousin, where fashion names were *made*. Nevertheless, the transition was difficult for Teddy; on more than one occasion, Gideon had discovered him at his massive mahogany desk, stabbing his Pimm's Cup with a cucumber spear and staring into space. *He absolutely needs a new project,* noted his concerned assistant. *This much was clear.*

The question was *who?*

Stepping lightly downstairs, the attentive assistant swept into the reception area, where two girls, one dark, the other fair, looked up from twin green-and-gold silk jacquard seats, their hands placidly folded on their crossed knees, their eyes alight with excitement.

"Mam'selles," he greeted them gravely.

Bing! Behind him, the gilded elevator doors shuddered to a halt. "Wait!" twittered a high-pitched, panicked voice. Their operator, Mr. Finch, unlatched the ornate brass gate, sliding it open with a clattering bang. Two girls, one tall, the other small (*with lapis lazuli for eyes,* noted Gideon) burst from the lift like crazed canaries.

"Sorry we're late," panted the silky-bobbed taller of the two. "We —"

"Got lost?" offered the dusky diva from her chair, pursing her voluptuous pout. The sylphlike blonde to her right elbowed her in the ribs.

"More like *distracted,*" smiled the petite brunette, gritting her pearly teeth. (In fact, instead of waiting out the Crescent Heights stoplight, Charlotte had decided to cut across a parking lot, ran over an orange cone, and chucked off a piece of her car — a detail she was *not* about to divulge now). "I mean, did you *see* the Mary

Had a Derek Lam display on the first floor? You'd remember if you had," she blurted before they could respond, clutching her most professional bright vermilion Hermès *grand modèle* agenda to her light gray ruffled chest. "That display is an absolute *work* of *art*," she breathed to Gideon. "Unlike *some* people, I can't walk by a masterpiece without taking time to admire it." Melissa's jaw dropped in protest, but Charlotte ignored her, cloyingly offering her hand. "I'm *sure* you understand, Mr. —"

"Peck," replied the solemn assistant.

"*Fabulous* to meet you!" Melissa nudged her frilly rival to the side, snatching Gideon's fig-and-cassis-lotioned hand from her grasp. "*Melissa Moon*. And can I just say," she continued, cocking a savagely gelled eyebrow in Charlotte's direction, "I don't think anyone who calls themselves fashion-conscious could *possibly* keep Mr. Pelligan waiting."

"He is . . . *here*, right?" Janie tentatively confirmed, allowing Charlotte and Melissa to lock in to a glare.

"Of course," Mr. Peck tipped into a quick, contrite bow, relieved to finally escort them up the gleaming marble staircase. As much as he abhorred their lowly emotional display, he also found it assuring. Miss Mary-Kate and Miss Ashley also bickered, and Teddy insisted it was a sign of talent.

Up they went, heels clacking — that is, until they reached the landing. The plush oriental carpet muted their footsteps, pair by pair, and they looked around. In contrast to the modern bustle downstairs — all pulsing beats, polished floors, and enticingly arranged collections — Mr. Pelligan's office brought to mind a centuries-old university or church. The vaulted ceiling gleamed like an empty eggshell, dark leather-bound books lined the hallway, and a gentle ticking filled the air. Two grandfather clocks — carved to resemble rockets? — flanked either side of Mr. Pelligan's daunting office door. Just as Gideon reached for the handle, they released a deep, internal whir, loudly clicked, and burst into song. The girls startled in alarm. Gideon did not react. Quite calmly, he pushed open the door, revealing at first the massive mahogany desk, and then, directly behind it . . .

The man.

"Listen to me!" He sang in perfect harmony with his clanging clocks. "*Don't listen to me.* Talk to me! *Don't talk to me.* Dance with me! *Don't dance with me.* NOOO . . . beep-beep!"

The four girls huddled together. (During their respective car rides home, they would have to agree: of all WTF moments, *this* was the WTF-est. It was seriously, like, should they *run*?) Several well-heeled members of his staff stood at either side of Mr. Pelligan's desk, hands behind their backs, staring straight ahead. It seemed Mr. Pelligan's musical outbursts, though tedious, were no cause for concern.

In fact, they were business as usual.

"Beep-beep!" He swiveled his high-seated ergonomic chair, bobbing up and down, and excitedly paddling the air. "Oooo . . .

bop. Do-do-do-do-do-do-do-do-fa! Fa! Fa! Fa! *Fashion*. Oooo . . . bop. Do-do-do-do-do-do-do-do-fa! Fa! Fa! Fa! *Fashion*."

The chiming melody ceased — but for a final reverberating note — and Mr. Pelligan settled back into his seat, sighing with satisfaction. "Those were a gift," he explained as the clocks resumed the more traditional duty of striking time. "From Mr. Bowie *himself*. Aren't they *marvelous*?"

Janie bit the insides of her cheeks. Mr. Bowie? As in *David* Bowie? As in the Thin White Duke? Was he freaking serious?

She could not *wait* to tell Amelia.

"Ah! My haute couture hatchlings," he greeted them at last, bulging his pale gray eyes. "Allow me to introduce you to my team." Pushing his chair back, Ted Pelligan grunted to his shining shoes. He wore a suit similar to the one he wore the Halloween night they first met, but in a different color — a lime green seersucker paired with a tie of lavender silk, a crisp white shirt, and traditional Ferragamo two-tone wing tips. Unlike Gideon and the rest of his staff, who boasted mannequin-perfect proportions, Teddy was short-limbed and stubby, with a round, protruding middle and two impossibly tiny feet. "I'm a *gummy bear*!" he'd sometimes wail, glimpsing his reflection.

(Before meetings, Gideon made sure to cover the mirrors.)

"My divine and diligent staff!" Mr. Pelligan beamed as his employees arranged themselves in V formation, Giddy at the head. "My faithful flock of Pelligans. *Mr. Peck*," he declared, indicating the solemn assistant, "you've already met. And, em" — he turned to the next employee in line with a blank, befuddled look — "em . . ."

"*Brian*, sir," the young man politely assisted him.

Mr. Pelligan gave him a cheerful slap on the back, moving on to the next in line, a stunning yellow-eyed girl with violet hair swept into a chain-metal chignon: "This is Dancer, and over here we have Prancer, *Dasher*, of course, Blitzen, Comet, and finally, yes" — he paused, returning to the young man with a dismissive sniff — "the unforgettable *Brian*. With his nose so bright."

A clap of his tidy hands, and all but one — a petite brunette, the woman he'd introduced as Prancer, who looked exactly like Natalie Portman, except with a lazy eye — filed through the exit. Sitting in a corner wing chair, she stared into her lap and proceeded to fold a piece of pale pink paper.

"*Wunderbar!*" The heavy wood door closed with a resounding boom, and Teddy flopped into his office chair, belting his hands across his belly. "Now." He swiveled around. "Can any of you tell me, what, thus far, you have learned?"

They hesitated, freezing into a line near the pin-striped fabric wall. How, exactly, were they expected to respond? Thus far we have learned that you, Ted Pelligan, are totally head-over-butt-heels crazy? And maybe, with our relative lack of quirk — with our bland, predictable sanity — we've already bored you to tears?

Janie had the sudden urge to throw a lamp, just to prove him wrong.

"Just *look* at them, Giddy!" Mr. Pelligan stopped midswivel, touching his assistant's arm. "Timid as *titmice*."

"Yes, sir."

"What you have learned!" He bounded to his miniature feet. "Is the *third* rule of Fashion. The *first*, of course, which you so *exemplarily* displayed this afternoon, is to *never* arrive *anywhere* on *time*."

"We're so sorry," Janie interrupted. "We —"

"The second!" he whispered, raising a finger to his lips. "*Never* apologize! And the third, which *I* so exemplarily displayed for *you* mere *moments* ago" — he bobbed two perfectly groomed silver eyebrows, an apparent signal to Mr. Peck, who quietly left the room — "*forget people's names*." He circled the stunned quartet, popping his gray eyes for emphasis. "As soon as you meet some- one — *pfffft!* That name should go flying out of your head. And if it *hasn't*, by all means, *pretend otherwise!*"

"But" — Petra paused, wondering if Mr. Pelligan's mushroomy shape had anything to do with his hallucinatory affect — "*why?*"

"Because that's *fashion*, my pouting pet!" Gesturing to a hang- ing black-and-white photograph of him and Madonna, he declared, "I've been calling *that* one Debbie for eighteen *years*. The woman bloody *worships* me. Copies my every move! You think she just *decided* to wear a nude satin conical bustier out of *nowhere?*" He tapped a fingernail against Madonna's young glass-framed face and narrowed his gray eyes. "I beg to differ."

Petra, Melissa, Janie, and Charlotte shared an uneasy glance.

No doubt a change of subject was in order, but all they could do was just *stand* there, like, lamely racking their brains. Wonky-eye Natalie was no help; she remained in the corner, staring into her lap and folding yet another piece of pink paper. When Gideon returned to the room carrying two lavender-striped hatboxes, the girls sighed their collective relief.

The dude's timing was impeccable.

"At last!" Mr. Pelligan brightened. A flutter of feet propelled him toward the corner of his massive mahogany desk where Gideon had placed the two hatboxes. "So," he winked. "Now that you know the *rules*" — he pried the top box open, dancing his fingers about the rim — "we may begin . . . the *game*."

He lifted the lavender lid high into the air, shaking it like a tambourine.

"The Trick-or-Treater!" Melissa gasped, recognizing the little handbag at once. And why wouldn't she? It was, after all, Poseur's first and only couture creation. Per Mr. Pelligan's request, they'd given it up for adoption. Even though he assured them the arrangement was temporary, in the back of their minds they wondered: would they ever see it again? Charlotte, Janie, and Petra gathered around as Melissa cradled the bag in her arms. It was all there: the electric-blue bamboo-silk material, the compact square Starburst shape, the board-short lace-up detail, *the interlocking gold P clasp.*

THE

TRICK

Color: "Atomic Turquoise"

gold chain/ribbon handle

gold zip closure

edges "stained" with diluted dye

Front Snap Pocket

purse profile – boardshort lace-up detail!

STARBURST SHAPED!!

OR TREATER

Janie   Furrish

Materials: bamboo/soy/cotton blend "silk" shell pleather interior

"Oo-oh," Melissa whinnied. "I've missed you so much!"

"Impossible," argued Mr. Pelligan, shuffling through a crisp stack of papers. Melissa gasped, clutching the handmade handbag to her chest.

"*Believe* me," Petra gave a roll of her tea green eyes. "She's *missed* that thing."

"My delightfully *duped* demoiselle," Mr. Pelligan sniffed. "I'm afraid I must insist — she did nothing of the kind."

Before they could continue arguing, a brief rustle of lavender tissue paper pulled their attention toward Gideon. "Perhaps *this*," the solemn assistant proposed, exhuming the second box's contents, "is the object of her yearning?"

The girls gaped in amazement, for Gideon had presented (it couldn't be!) the *Trick-or-Treater*. Was it some kind of magic trick? Had he pickpocketed Melissa's handbag from under her MAC-powdered nose, leaving in its place a twitching white rabbit?

"I —" Melissa looked between the Trick-or-Treater in her arms and the one in Gideon's hand, dumbfounded. "I —"

"My thoughts *precisely*!" agreed Mr. Pelligan, clasping his hands to his chest. "It's *quite* the little copy, if I say so myself. But, then again, I say everything myself." He giggled, quickly collected himself, and handed them each an official-looking packet from his desk. "As soon as we have your *permission* — and I do mean signing this *contract*, my legally-bound lovelies — we'll begin *production*, manufacturing not *one* handbag, not *two* handbags, but" — he turned to his solemn assistant with a flutter of eyelids — "Giddy. What *was* our final number?"

"One thousand, sir."

"One," Janie rasped, clutching Charlotte's cashmere-covered arm for support, "*thousand*?"

"Chin up, up!" Mr. Pelligan clucked. "In time, we'll be producing them by the *tens* of thousands. Isn't that right, em" — he pinched the bridge of his nose and snapped his small fingers — "you there!"

At last, the Natalie look-alike looked up (well, at least *one* eye looked up — the other stared fiercely to the left). Quickly, she got to her feet, forgetting a collection of three or four pink origami cranes that spilled from her lap to the floor.

"Em . . ." Teddy grimaced, snapping his fingers.

"*Birdie,*" she piped up, following him with her good eye as he drifted toward his desk. "Birdie *Pelligan*?" she clarified, hoping to ring a bell.

"Oh yes, yes, *Birdie*. Apple of my eye, fruit of my loins." He brushed her off, picking up the phone. "Do your *jobbie*, won't you, darling?"

With a resigned sigh, Birdie nodded, refocusing on the four girls (that is, her *right* eye focused; the other kind of veered off to gawk at a stained-glass Tiffany lamp). "Please," she said with a brave smile, indicating a group of four British colonial cushioned wicker chairs. "Sit."

They sat, sharing their umpteenth wondering look. Wonky-eye was Mr. Pelligan's *daughter*? Maybe he'd adopted her from

Romania or something. Or assumed the form of a bull and raped a tree branch, like Zeus.

"The Trick-or-Tritterer," she began, winced, and darted a worried eye toward her father. But he was already absorbed by his phone call, oblivious to her blunder. "The *Trick-or-Treater*," she breathed a sigh of relief, starting again, "if handled well — and we at Ted Pelligan handle *everything* well — will positively *shake* the fashion industry. But before the big shake, we need the *shimmies*. Fashion *foreshocks*, if you will. How, you ask? We'd like to propose a *celebriteaser*." Noting their baffled expressions, she paused. "Are you, um, familiar with that term?"

Janie, Petra, and Charlotte glanced Melissa's way. She *was* their Director of Public Relations, after all; wasn't it *her* responsibility to know?

Melissa arced a cocky eyebrow, and cleared her throat. "Eeyea . . . no."

"Wow," Birdie breathed, grinning at the floor. She wasn't used to knowing *more* than other people. It made her feel funny inside. "Don't worry." She looked up, still grinning. "Celebriteaser is an easy one. It's just, like, famous people — that's the *celebrity* part — who show off the latest whatever-it-is *before anyone else* — that's the *tease* part. Take Kate Moss," she suggested, getting into her stride. "When she appeared in a pair of wide-leg vintage Chloé jeans — and this at the *height* of skinny jean popularity — everyone *had* to know: *What* are they? *Where* are they? And importantly, how soon can *they* be *mine*?"

"I bought a pair," Charlotte admitted, omitting the small detail that she never wore them (they totally gave her elephant butt). "I couldn't resist."

"Me too," Petra confessed.

"Oh, Miss I-Never-Buy-Designer," Melissa chided her.

"They're *vintage!*" Petra blushed, but she knew as well as Melissa: the excuse was pretty weak. "I don't know what it is," she moaned. "Kate Moss has this, like, *power* over me."

"I know," Birdie intoned, widening her good eye. "She has that power over everybody. When Kate wears a Ted Pelligan original, our sales spike through the roof. But fashion-wise, she's entirely independent — can't be bought, won't do favors. *Believe me,* I've tried." The Pelligan marketing director sighed, clasping her hands. "Once, I prayed."

"*That's* our promotion strategy?" Melissa worried aloud, still clutching the Treater to her lap. "Praying to Kate Moss?"

"Heavens, no." Birdie wonked her eye open. "Kate Moss is the exception, but *most* celebrities have a price. And we at Ted Pelligan are willing to pay it. *Your* bag on the *right* starlet's arm?" She clucked her tongue, and smiled. "Poseur could be the biggest P since Prada."

Janie, Melissa, Charlotte, and Petra shivered with excitement, grinning with anticipation. It *was* Prada, after all, who'd all but banned them *for life* from their Rodeo store (okay, so they'd happened to host a launch party that got the *teensiest* bit out of control). That Ted Pelligan was going to carry *one thousand* Treaters was freakin' crazy *enough*. But snagging Prada's crown as fashion's reigning Queen P?

It was almost, like, too P to picture.

"I think I speak for the rest of us that a celebriteaser is the right way to go," Melissa blurted, breaking the dream-filled silence.

"Do you know who it's going to be?" Janie turned to Birdie, almost too thrilled to speak. Quickly, she checked her dorktastic enthusiasm, pursing her lips like the poor man's Posh.

"We're working on that," Birdie assured her, checking in with Mr. Pelligan. Noticing her inquisitive glance, he raised a well-buffed hold-a-moment finger.

"Darling," he said into the phone. "I say this with *absolute* love — white is *not* your color. Yes, I know it was your wedding. Well, you looked positively *contagious*. Yes. Yes. Well, you'll know better next time, won't you? All right. Love you, too. Kiss-kiss. Ciao-ciao. Ciao."

He clattered the old-fashioned ivory receiver into the polished gold cradle and wiped his hand on his lavender pant leg, eyeing the phone with disdain. "Yicchh!" he lamented. "An absolute *nightmare!*"

Birdie beamed, always thrilled by her father's ire (as long as it wasn't directed at her). "Jessica?" she guessed.

"Messica," he groused in reply. Gideon chuckled softly to himself, crouched to the floor, and pinched a pink paper crane into his lap. The girls, meanwhile, surged with curiosity. *Jessica who?* Jessica Alba? Jessica Simpson? Jessica Biel? Or maybe, due to Mr.

Pelligan's nasty industry habit, her name wasn't Jessica at all. Oh, *who was it*? And most important . . .

Was *she* their celebriteaser?

"So," Mr. Pelligan launched his ergonomic chair backward and swiveled around. "Birdie's apprised you of our plan for takeoff?"

"They want to know *who*," his daughter jumped in before they could respond. "I said I'd have to check with you first."

"We'll make our decision in precisely one week." Mr. Pelligan got to his feet and stretched. "Friday, as they say, is *fly* day. We'll have to secure the right *stage*, of course."

"Stage?" Melissa piped up, eyes shining. As with any exhibitionist, the word "stage" had a near physical effect on her. Like saying "open bar" to an alcoholic or "playground" to Michael Jackson.

"Of *course* a stage!" Mr. Pelligan harrumphed. "If Kate Moss had worn her Chloés in the privacy of her own *opium den*, do you think we would have ever known the difference? Of course not! Celebriteasers need to get out, *out*. Into the public *eye* — and by eye, of course, I mean *lens*."

"Paparazzi," Birdie explained, succumbing again to that funny, secret feeling. "That's what a stage is. Any place with paparazzi."

"No stage but the *world* stage will do," Mr. Pelligan emphasized. "I won't rest until the Treater's featured in every magazine from *US Weekly* to *Bosnian Vogue*!"

"Omigod!" Melissa gasped, clapping a manicured hand to her

mouth. "Sorry, but . . . I have the *perfect* event." Belting it out like Oprah, she exclaimed, "My dad's *engagement partyyyyy*!"

"Your" — Ted Pelligan fluttered his silver lashes in abject distaste — "*dad?*"

"It's not like that," Charlotte assured him in the blasé tone of a girl whose *own* actor/director/producer dad, Hollywood icon Bud Beverwil, all but out-famoused the world. She widened her pool green eyes and tried to sound impressed. "Her dad is Seedy *Moon*."

"*No.*" Mr. Pelligan melted into a smile. "You mean that angry-looking chap with the tattoos and the gold chains — Giddy, what *do* they call these newfangled urban bards?"

"Rap stars, sir."

"Rap stars," he rhapsodized, once again trilling his *r*'s. "You mean to say," he addressed Melissa, "in addition to *profane* and *rudimentary* verse, these '*rrrrap* stars' produce *daughters*? And one of these daughters is you?"

"That's right," she happily confirmed, crossing her legs.

"Tut-tut, my sweet," he stopped her, reached into a file, and retrieved a perfectly trimmed newspaper clipping. Holding it as far away from his face as possible, he blinked behind his rimless rectangular eyewear and gazed down his small, rounded nose. " 'In honor of his fiancée's favorite *color*, hip-hop mogul Seedy *Moon* will host an all-night Pink Party at his Bel Air *estate*, scheduled for the first Saturday of *December*. The budget, rumored to have surpassed the two-million-*dollar* mark, has divided fans into two *camps*. "It's the American Dream, right?" laughs Benita Baker, a grocery clerk in Echo Park. "He came from nothing, just like me." "Pathetic," argues Duck Meaney, a self-described Columbia dropout sipping a four-dollar cappuccino outside Mäni's Bakery in Venice Beach. "This is a country humbled by economic crisis. The people should rise up and storm his Bel Air estate with torches." Mr. Moon, however, makes *no* apologies. "What can I say," he grinned at reporters. "I'm in love. I out-Diddy'd myself." ' "

"That was the *L.A. Times.*" Melissa beamed, uncrossing and recrossing her long, legging-clad legs. "Did you see the write-up in *Vanity Fair?* They mention me in that one."

"Of all the most *delightful* coincidences." Mr. Pelligan lowered the clipping to his polished mahogany desk and removed his glasses. "You must know . . . I keep a file for ideal stages, and your father's engagement party made the top five."

"I already *asked*," Birdie blurted in a panic, her left eye lolling toward her nose. If her father found out she'd forgotten to make the call, he'd take away her riding privileges! "*Four* times," she elaborated her lie. "Mr. Moon's assistant told me if I called again he'd have me arrested!"

"*Jerome* told you that?" Melissa gaped. *That cornrowed clown declined a call from Ted Pelligan? Was he looking to get fired?* Darting worried black eyes toward Mr. Pelligan, Melissa quickly shook her head. "Please, don't listen to that fool, Mr. Pelligan. My dad would be *honored* to work with you. For real."

"Hear that, *Buttercup?*" Mr. Pelligan arced an eyebrow at his deceitful daughter, pointedly evoking her pony's name. "Mr. Moon would be . . . *honored*."

As Birdie retired to her chair to glumly fold another piece of pink paper, Mr. Pelligan escorted the four girls to the door. "Well, my fashionista fledglings, I *did* have several stages swimming about, but if the Moon fete is what you *want*, the Moon fete is what you *get*. In the meantime, if you'll just allow me to put on my *chapeau à penser*, I'll choose the *perfect* celebriteaser. And she *must* be perfect! You are official protégées *Pelligan*, my lovelies, and if *I* get the best, *you* get the best. *Bon!*" The silver-haired tycoon clapped his hands together, tipping into a brisk bow. "I hope this meeting was as *gorgeous* a pleasure for you as it was for me."

"Completely," Charlotte assured him, extending her small hand. "We cannot wait until Friday, Mr. . . . um . . ." She repressed a smile. "Mr. . . ."

"Oh!" Petra leapt to her friend's assistance, only to cover her mouth and frown. *"You* know." She tapped her foot. *"Agh*, it's *totally* on the tip of my tongue."

"Something with a *P*?" Melissa suggested.

"I think it was a *D*," Janie contradicted.

"Oh, Mr. *Dunderplotzer*!" Charlotte blurted, daring to meet Mr. Pelligan's eye; to her relief, it twinkled back — so proud!

"My dear little understudies," he declared, hoarse with emotion. "Together we will go so far!"

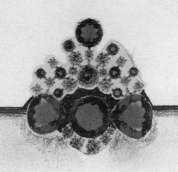

If red stands for passion
and white for what's pure
then a mix of the two
stands for the cure
to all of our woes
talkin' 'bout LOVE (haha)
so come all yee thugz
come all yee ho's
and don't even think
tonight all colors in life
will be
PINK

The Girl: Vivien Ho
The Getup: Sapphire blue Akiko silk top, Hudson shiny black skinny jeans, metallic-gold jeweled thong sandals by Manolo Blahnik, white patent tassled hobo by Ho Bag

By the time Melissa dropped Petra off at her pillared peach Beverly Hills estate on Lexington Road, filled her tank with premium gas, told the gas attendant to "*get* that *squeegee* outta my *face*," and made it back to her glass-glinting cliff-side Bel Air estate, it was already after seven o'clock. Spotless white vans and black town cars crowded the circular drive, declaring their intentions in various calligraphic fonts: Wolfgang Puck Catering, Paradise Gardens Landscaping Design, Rex Covington Ice Sculpture, Ben Stanton Lighting Design, Rita Flora Flower Arrangements, Fireworks by Orlando Special Effects. Melissa wasn't impressed. Not only did navigating the Lexus through this pre-party obstacle course add an *extra* five minutes to her commute, but *one* of these four-wheeled jokers — a bright pink Mini-Pooper, of course — had the *nerve* to jack her spot. *Yvette* — the white adhesive letters pranced across the back windshield — *Professional Romantician*. Melissa crinkled her nose. *Romantician?* What the *eff* was that? And did "Yvette" *not* see the polished brass *Reserved for M. M.* plaque on the wall, or was "Yvette" plain *blind*?

But, no — deep breath — she was too happy to be mad. The meeting with Ted Pelligan had actually surpassed her high expectations. True, he was kind of a freak, but wasn't that precisely the point? This was *fashion*! *All* the major players were freaks: Karl Lagerfeld with his untakeoffable black terminator shades, Donatella Versace with her trout mouth and radioactive blond Barbie hair, Marc Jacobs with his on-and-off addictions to cocaine and Scottish plaid skorts, Naomi Campbell, um . . . hello?

Crazy was, like, a freakin' *credential*.

"I'm home!" She danced into the Moons' ultramodern kitchen, dropping her bulging fuchsia Marc Jacobs Stam satchel on the polished slate floor. Her ever-pursuant Pomeranian, Emilio Poochie, skidded to a halt, told the bag off in two barks (from now on, *I'm* the one she carries. You *feel* me, punk?), and tore off in a crazed streak. His mistress was *excited*. Which meant — wait, did it? Yes, it did! — *he* was excited! Good, 'cause he *totally* had this awesome new routine worked out. First, he'd bark holy rabies. Then he'd spin around really fast, collide into a wall, and finally? He'd bite the crazy fluff-wand sticking out of his butt.

For some reason, that was a major crowd pleaser.

"Omigod, Emilio, calm *down*!" Melissa laughed, scooping her favorite tan-and-white fur ball into her arms and hugging him to her pillowy double D's. "You are so crazy!" she squealed, tickling his belly.

"Melissa, you are *working* him *up*." Vivien Ho, her father's six-foot-tall biatch of a fiancée, grimaced from across the light gray marble-topped kitchen island. As usual, her top — a flimsy sapphire blue silk Akiko number, which she'd no doubt chosen to make her violet contacts pop — provided a way-more-than-necessary glimpse of the bronzered canyon between her jutting breasts (or as Melissa preferred to call it: Silicone Valley). Her mouth (which, let's be honest, was less a mouth than a pink-frosted collagen donut) gaped wide open. She looked like one of those low-rent carnival amusements, you know: *Throw a ball into the clown's mouth! Win a prize!* Of course, in this case, the ball was an eighteen-carat diamond. The prize was Vivien herself. And Melissa's father? *The lucky winner.*

Yeah. The irony wasn't lost on Melissa, either.

"Yvette!" Vivien refocused her attention to her buzzing Black-Berry, snatching it to her diamond-dribbling ear. "Yeah. Uh-huh. Oh, you're in the master bathroom?"

Seedy Moon and his falling-apart grayish Bugs Bunny slippers shuffled into the kitchen, and Melissa skipped a circle around the kitchen island (no easy feat in five-inch Louboutins) and shrieked, clapping her manicured hands. "Sure, I can come upstairs," Vivien scowled, pressing a dragon-red fingernail to her ear. "I'll be there in a second."

"Whattup?" Seedy braced himself as his fiancée clapped her phone shut, fluttered her false lashes shut, and set her jaw in a way that meant one thing: *drama.*

"Seedy, I swear to God." She scooted her bar stool back and clacked her gold metallic jeweled thong sandals to the polished slate floor. "That dog *better* be out of here by the time I get back. I am on my *last nerve*."

As Melissa and Emilio joyfully joint-freaked her abandoned bar stool, she threw her gleaming shoulders back, click-clacked across the floor, and exited in a righteous huff. Seedy followed her apoplectic apple-butt with a mingled look of concern and (he couldn't help himself) admiration, pushing some air between his full lips.

"Daddy!" his daughter's cheerful voice rose behind him. "I *have* to talk to you!"

"Yeah, baby." He turned around, attempting a smile. He'd been dreading this conversation all afternoon, holing up like a coward in his soundproof glass meditation room. For two hours he did nothing but contemplate his meditation moat — watching the koi fish do their thing and listening to Chopin's nocturnes. Yeah, that's right: *classical music.* Ever since he'd hired Melissa's Special Studies adviser, Lena, to play piano for the Pink Party, he found himself programming Mozart into his iPod instead of Mos Def. *Some of this powdered wig shit ain't so bad,* he admitted to himself in semishock.

But he couldn't stay in the glass room forever.

"Listen . . ." Seedy sighed, reeling his only daughter in for a big hug and pancaking poor Emilio in the process. The little Pomeranian squirmed, crazier than a squirrel in a bag of nuts. "I know how much you were looking forward to this day, and . . . I wish I didn't have to tell you this, but . . ." He sighed again, released her from the hug, and took a small step backward. Emilio plopped in a heap to the gleaming floor. "The results are inconclusive," he informed her gently but firmly, gripping the backs of her arms.

Melissa blinked. *Results?* What was he talking about? Moments later, her mind reoriented like a Magic 8 Ball after a firm shake, and the answer floated to the surface. *Oh . . .*

He was talking about *the tag.*

Back in September, as part of their now notorious launch party, she, Petra, Charlotte, and Janie had hosted a Name Our Label contest. They'd collected over a hundred suggestions from an equal number of guests, all of them written on two-by-one-inch white clothing tags. The tags had been locked into a custom-made clear globe safe—but "safe" they most definitely were not. Someone had broken into the globe. Someone had *tagged* the *tags*, defacing each one with a single word.

Poseur.

As a personal message to the vandal, they named their label in honor of the insult. Seedy called this "appropriating the language of the oppressor," but his daughter wasn't going to stop. "My business has been *violated*," she'd protested, startling him awake from a nap. "And it's gonna take a lot more than the I'm-Rubber-You're-Glue defense for me to get over that. Until I know *who* the vandal is — until I *bring* that fool to *justice* — I will not, nay, I *cannot* move on."

Her father, who'd been hiding behind his Relax the Back

Swedish neck cushion, agreed to see what he could do.

Unfortunately, lack of evidence worked against them; it wasn't until eighth-grader Nikki Pellegrini miraculously discovered one of the vandalized tags in a garbage-art installation that Melissa could finally kick off two major orders of business. First, immediately appoint Nikki Poseur's new intern (she'd need to keep that eagle eye close). Second, give the treasured tag to her father, who would in turn give it to *the Man in K-Town*. Melissa didn't know much about *the Man in K-Town*, except, a) he was number 9 on her dad's speed-dial, and b) he took care of business, all *kinds* of business. "No man better than *my* Man at graffiti interpretation," her father assured her. "One week with that tag a yours? Culprit's good as *cuffed*."

All of which brings us back to the Moons' ultramodern kitchen, where tasteful ambient lighting illuminated the cool stainless steel appliances, the dark slate floors, the spotless glass cabinets, the light gray marble countertops . . . and Melissa's beautiful yet dismayed face.

"*Inconclusive?*" she squawked, braiding her body-buttered arms across her voluptuous chest. "What does that mean, 'the results are *inconclusive*'?"

Seedy threw up his hands, equally incredulous. "It means he couldn't figure it out!"

"But the Man in K-Town has a *zero percent fail rate*," Melissa reminded him, stomping her stiletto. "You *said*."

"I know!" Seedy admitted, shaking his head, clearly perplexed.

"Okay." Melissa steepled her hands under her chin, fluttering her Dior Iconic-coated lashes shut. "Just tell me what he said. Like, *exactly* what he said."

Seedy stuttered a zebra-upholstered bar stool under his Adidas tracksuited butt and sat. "He said he couldn't tell much from the handwriting. The perpetrator purposely wrote in block letters, the pen was a generic Sharpie . . . nothing distinctive. No fingerprints. He sent the tag to a lab for chemical analysis. Nothing there either . . ." He trailed off, losing himself in thought. "Except . . . "

"Except *what?*" Melissa gripped the gray marble countertop. "Daddy!"

Squeezing the back of his neck, Seedy gazed at the floor, still shaking his head. His deep brown eyes flicked upward.

"He said he found traces of *sea kelp*."

"*Sea* kelp," Melissa repeated after a beat of baffled silence. She crumpled her brow. "You mean, like . . . seaweed?"

"Man, I'm starting to wonder . . ." Her father cringed, squeezing the back of neck. "Maybe K-Town's losing his *touch?*"

An unsympathetic Melissa shrugged, sucking the insides of her cheeks.

"I mean," he continued pensively. "Who are we supposed to believe broke into your contest?" Bugging out his eyes, he stuck out his tongue and splayed his bejeweled fingers. "*Swamp* thing?"

Despite herself, Melissa giggled. "*Stupid,*" she chastised him, pushing his powerful shoulder. He captured her lemon-and-sage-moisturized hand, giving it a gentle squeeze.

"It's gonna be okay."

"It is?"

"No doubt," he assured her. "When something bad happens, you just got to think — this is going to make some room for something good."

Melissa gently smiled. Sometimes her dad's Buddha-bytes actually made sense. "I guess I can see that."

"You can?" Seedy bobbed his eyebrows, impressed with himself. "Oh, wait a minute," he remembered, slapped his knees, and grinned. "You had your big *meeting* today, right? How'd it go?"

"Well . . ." Melissa bit her Smashbox-lacquered lower lip, her early excitement returning in a throb. From his collapsed position on the floor, Emilio Poochie lifted his head, perking up his ears. "Ted Pelligan is really serious about us, Daddy. I mean . . . he's even arranging a celebriteaser."

Before Seedy had a chance to respond, Vivien materialized at the kitchen entrance, poised like a cobra above her jeweled metallic sandals. "He's giving you a *what*?"

Melissa arced her perfectly gelled eyebrow. "You heard me."

"Melissa," Seedy frowned as Vivien clattered to his side. *"Watch* your —"

"I don't believe you," his fiancée huffed at his daughter before he could finish, narrowing her violet eyes. Planting a hand on her hip, she pursed her pink-frosted collagen donut into an impressive-looking twist pastry. "What could you have possibly done to deserve a celebriteaser?"

"What could *I* have done?" Melissa rasped with laughter. As if Vivien's totally tacky designer handbag company, Ho Bag, had anything to do with hard work. *Melissa* was the one who toiled to get her business off the ground, pulling herself up by her own Manolo Blahnik *bootstraps*, while Vivien just kicked up her heels, coasting by on the Moon name. Contrary to the claims of her sham memoir, *The Audacity of Ho*, the woman did not do an *ounce* of work — unless you counted X'ing a few forms once a month.

Melissa was *this close* to X'ing Vivien's freeloading face.

"I'd just like to say," she began.

"YO!" her father boomed, rattling the china in the nearest glass cabinet and shutting her up in an instant. Emilio ejected through the archway exit like a piece of shrapnel. "Thank you for your attention!" he boomed again, obliterating the sound of the tiny dog clattering down the hall. "Will one of you please be so kind as to tell me what a celebriteaser mother-McMuffin *is* before I lose my mother-McMuffin *mind*?"

"A celebriteaser," Melissa and Vivien began together. After a strained pause, the fake-baked fiancée continued.

"Baby, remember last month? When A-Rod was spotted on Madison drinking MoonWater?"

At MoonWater, Seedy relaxed into a smile. He couldn't help himself. After languishing on the Whole Foods shelves for more than three months, sales for his bottled mineral water—the latest effort to diversify and expand the Moon brand—had finally started to pick up.

"That's a celebriteaser," Melissa explained, happy to show off her new knowledge. "As soon as people saw A-Rod drinking it, it was like, *buh-ham*! They started buying."

"Uh, *excuse* me," protested Seedy, pointing a bejeweled finger. "People started *buying* because we are the *only* water that uses a patented *moon rock* filtration *process*." He waited for them to argue, crumpling his brow like an accordion. *"Thank you,"* he nodded, interpreting their cowed silence as victory. "Now" — he returned to his daughter — "you tellin' me A-Rod agreed to walk down Madison holdin' a *purse*?"

"Daddy, no!" Melissa leaned against the kitchen island and laughed. "A *girl* celebrity's gonna to do it, obvie."

"Who?" Vivien ventured, trying to sound casual, but clearly *dying* to know. Melissa smirked, triumphant.

"We find out in a week. And, I was thinking, because the timing's so perfect . . ." She clasped her hands, squinched her nose, and turned in her ankle, achieving the pinnacle of pigeon-toed cuteness. "Daddy? We can we do it at the Pink Party, right?"

Her father had this habit: right before he gave her what he wanted, he winked his left eye. Melissa could see it happening, but — just as his left cheek began cinching into its corresponding eyelid — Vivien landed her hand on his knee.

"No," she said, grinding the wink to a halt, and punctuated her coup with a pert toss of her spiraling, waist-length jet-black extensions. A resulting *whoosh* of *Frédéric Fekkai* Sheer Hold hair-spray hovered in the air, hypnotizing her fiancé. "This party is an *intimate affair*," she continued, giving his knee a squeeze. "Between our family and *closest* friends."

"Wait — what?" Melissa began to panic. Her father was puckering his mouth in that she-has-a-good-point way, which was completely *not* okay. "We invited over five hundred people," she reminded him, returning to Vivien in a flash. "And don't *even* try to tell me *Tila Tequila* counts as a 'close friend.' "

"Tila Tequila," Vivien ruffled in retort, "and I are *very* close friends. We go back to Ho Bag's Beverly Center Grand Opening. Of *course* she deserves an invitation!"

"Daddy," Melissa trembled in a valiant attempt to repress her mounting rage. Even the *words* "Ho Bag" pummeled her patience like a one-two punch. "Don't you see what's happening? The only reason she doesn't want me to hold the celebriteaser at the Pink Party is because she doesn't want *Poseur* to take attention away from *Ho Bag*."

"Is that true?" Seedy faced his fiancée with concern.

"Of course not!" Vivien gasped, pressing her hand to her heart. "How can you even *ask* me that?"

"Vee," he apologized, reaching for her gold-bangled arm. "You know, I . . ."

"Listen." She turned to address Melissa directly, her violet eyes growing glassy. "You are the daughter of the love of my *life*. And I am *proud* of your accomplishments. All I'm asking is for one night. For you, me, *and* your dad to put career stuff *aside* and take the *time* to honor what's important."

Melissa frowned at the floor, tracing the outline of a polished slate tile with the metallic toe of her shoe. The sincerity in Vivien's tone had her totally buggin'. It couldn't be Vivien's feelings were actually *hurt*, could it?

It couldn't be Vivien had actual *feelings*?

"This is a celebration of our *love*," Seedy's fiancée continued, hand still on her heart. "And — I know you don't believe me, but — you are *so* part of that love, Melissa. Don't you *know* that?"

Melissa set her jaw and refused to look up, tracing and retracing the slate tile with her toe. She knew what she must look like. Like a spoiled brat. But she *wasn't*.

Was she?

"Well," Seedy breathed, patting his emotional fiancée on her silk-draped back. "Friends-and-family-only sure as heck gets *my* vote."

"But . . ." His daughter looked up and gaped.

"No celebriteasers," he reprimanded sternly. "That's final."

In the great haystack of unfairness, her father's I'm-so-disappointed-in-you tone was the last and final straw. Melissa exploded into tears, jerked her stool back, and bolted from the room. "Fine!" she cried from down the spacious hall, slamming the heavy oak door. A framed photograph of her father and Snoop Dogg at the Grammys quaked on the wall and crashed loudly to the floor, fracturing in three places. Melissa crouched to her knees, tearfully picking up the pieces. *I really am a spoiled brat,* she realized. *A bad seed. The reason things suck.* In the words of Alec Baldwin: *a thoughtless little pig.*

In comparison to me, she grew nauseous with shame, *Vivien's probably a saint.*

The Guy: Evan Beverwil
The Getup: Tokyo tan Quiksilver Oxford Weekend pants, black My Morning Jacket Evil Urges Owl tee, black Havaiana flip-flops, tattoo: to be determined

The summer before freshman year his mom called him into the kitchen where she was sitting at the table with her interior designer (the *supremely* doable Heidi Meister) and was, like, "Evan, we're redecorating your room." At first he was all, *I like my room the way it is,* but then Heidi smiled, reached across the table — she was wearing this super tight white V-neck so he could see the outline of her bra — and said, "Evan, sweetheart. I one-hundred-percent *promise* to work *only* within the bounds of your personal ass static."

He must have misheard though, 'cause his mom just sat there calmly tying her hair into a bun, which he pretty much figured she would *not* be doing if Heidi had just said what he'd *thought* she'd said. Still, it was pretty deadly: Heidi's t-shirt + Heidi's killer Southern accent + the whole *idea* of "ass static" = sending his system into total overdrive. *"Do whatever you want,"* he'd practically shouted, and got the hell out of there.

Well, for a solid three years he'd regretted that decision, and never more deeply than right now. Charlotte had just come home from that business meeting thing of hers, and judging by the high-pitched frequency of girl noise downstairs, she wasn't alone.

Under normal circumstances, he'd grimace in pain, retreating into his room to blast some Tom Petty — purify his ears. *This* time, however, he turned the music down, cracked his door open, and cautiously leaned into the hall.

"What about when he was like, oh, yeah, *Madonna!*" A girl's voice gaspingly squeaked, trying to get the words out. "That *bustier* . . . was so . . . *mine!*"

She and his sister dissolved into laughter, and Evan swiftly closed his bedroom door, leaning against it. There was no mistaking that voice.

Janie Farrish was in his house.

Not to say she'd never been inside his house before. There was that one time when school just started and Charlotte was like, "Distract her," for whatever reason. Of course, he'd only been too happy to oblige, tromping downstairs in his bare feet, big grin on his face, all ready to get his game on, or whatever. *What a douche,* he cringed at the memory. Talking to cute girls might be his forte, but "beating fortes into fairy dust" — that was Janie's. Because she was more than just *cute,* you know? She was smart, and cool, and funny, and . . . man.

She *was* pretty effin' cute.

But she barely even *looked* at him, let alone talked to him. Not to say there hadn't been *hints* of progress. Like, that one night at the La Brea Tar Pits when she was all, "In second grade the tour guide told me the elephant statue was real," and he was all, "I had nightmares about that elephant," and she was all, "Me too!" and they laughed. That was cool. Or the time she spilled her drawings and he helped pick them up and she thanked him with those moody gray ocean eyes of hers. *Man.* That was awesome. But they were always just *moments*, you know? And then she'd get this look on her face — like his buddy Theo when he ate something and was all, "Dude, are there *peanuts* in this?!" and fisted his tongue with a napkin because he was allergic. Yeah. That was her expression. She'd be, like, *Bye*, and hightail it out of there, wherever "there" happened to be, which was to say, wherever *he* happened to be, which was to say, wherever she didn't want to be.

It wasn't his style to get into details, but for the sake of argument: how epically shiteous was their *last* interaction? For some tard-*tastic* reason, he actually thought she'd be *down* to design his tattoo — and maybe they'd get to know each other. But no. As usual, she'd been all *blah* about it. Like the way she kept drifting in and out of conversation, checking herself out in his car window. It was like, come *on*. He'd been *this close* to grabbing her by the shoulders, like, "Listen. You are as drop-dead gorgeous now as you were two seconds ago. Could you *please* just *focus* before I lose my shit?"

The thing was — and he guessed this was pretty messed up, *but* — the whole "getting rejected" thing? It was kind of *addicting*. For as long as he could remember, girls had been pretty, you know . . . available. The phrase "shooting fish in a barrel" came to mind, but no — even that involved a *little* effort. All he had to do was, like, *walk up* to the barrel. *Maybe* look inside. After that, the fish kind of just died. Like, of their own free will. And these were *quality* fish too. Like *models*, and shit.

So why did Janie hate him so hard? Another eruption of girl noise, followed by a percussive round of encroaching footsteps, cued him to back step into his room and swiftly close the door. A few seconds later, the footsteps floated past his door, headed down the hall. His sister's bedroom door creaked open, and Janie said, "You really think so?" Then the door swung back, clicked shut, and it was quiet. He sighed.

Why did the hate make her so hot?

But no, he would *not* talk to her. The time had come to end this humiliation parade. He scanned his room for some kind of diversion: the half-finished take-home Algebra II quiz on his desk, the MacBook on the shelf *above* his desk, the *Pineapple Express* DVD on the floor *by* his desk. Wait. Combine those last two things with a certain something *inside* his desk?

He had a pretty decent excuse for the next two hours.

Crouching to his weathered boardwalk-style hardwood floor, he shimmied his bottom desk drawer open, pushed aside a rumpled black sweatshirt, and curved his fingers around a familiar, cool column of glass.

To choosing your addictions, he thought, and raised the bong into the air.

The Girl (sort of): Don John
The Getup: White Dolce & Gabbana Magic-Fit pants, Dirty English by Juicy Couture black-and-white argyle sweater vest, Penguin Secret Utopia Mopia shirt, white Converse by John Varvatos, black Gucci messenger bag, and organic pearl quinoa, "Soul Food of the Andes," by Alter Eco

"That's *it*!" Charlotte's pot-bellied but perky neighbor, fashion adviser, and self-described "kindred spirit" burst into her spacious bedroom. An ornate scarlet Chinese fan fluttered under his baby-smooth, foundation-slathered chin, the only splash of color in an otherwise black-and-white ensemble: white pants, gray-and-white abstract-print shirt, a black-and-white cashmere argyle vest, pearl white knotted silk neck scarf, and the *pièce de résistance*, a white Juicy Couture glimmer wool newsboy cap. "I am in a category five tizzy," he panted. "This tizzy can*not* be tamed."

"*Pourquoi?*" Charlotte looked up from the Ted Pelligan Christmas catalog she and Janie had been perusing on her sun-dappled four-poster mahogany bed, and Janie watched on, mystified. Was it normal for bug-eyed, unabashedly bronzered boys to burst at random into her bedroom? "What *happened*?" Charlotte twinkled merrily, widening her thickly lashed chlorine eyes.

With a jerk of his wrist, the butterfly-bright fan clapped together.

"*Morticia* happened," he breathed, referring, of course, to Mort, the ancient wheelchair-bound retired Hollywood producer to whom, in exchange for luxury guesthouse living and twenty-four-hour pool access, he'd sold his tender bohemian soul. As a small act of rebellion, Don John referred to his master only by nickname — assigning one to each of his myriad moods: Mort-hog for his emotional-eating days, Morgie-Porgie for his crybaby days, Mortata for his sassy days, Auntie M for his gassy days, Moriah for his diva days, and, lastly, *Morticia* . . . for his out-to-obliterate-what-remaining-shreds-of-sanity-Don-John-has-left days.

"Oh no . . ." Charlotte observed her flustered friend from under a delicate, knitted brow. "Is he making you *work* for a living?"

Don John slid his black aviator sunglasses to the tip of his nose and squinted. *"Dawn,"* he barked in what Janie guessed was a not-so-good imitation of Mort's Long Island accent. "Where the *hell* is my remote?! Wait-ta-minute. Is the *heat* on? How many times do I have to tell you, NO HEAT. I need some of that tea, what-tis-it, you know what I mean — the *digestion* kind! Wait-ta-minute . . . I can't feel the left side of my face. Dawn? Dawn! DAWN!!!" The nineteen-year-old aspiring actor collapsed into Charlotte's pale green velvet chaise longue and flailed a doughy yet tan arm behind him. "Gaahahahah!" He quietly affected a sob. "I thought he'd never *stop*!"

As Charlotte slid off the frothy yellow and mint meringue four-poster bed, Janie tucked her foot under her butt and smiled. If Charlotte or Don John happened to glance her way, she'd want to look relaxed, amused, and, well, *included* — which is to say, the opposite of how she felt (which is to say, ignored).

"Poor Don John." Charlotte oozed, gazing into the oval gilded mirror above her flickering fireplace. She curved her delicate arms into a lazy arabesque, teasing a lacquered black pin from her all-business bun. "You're here now," she reminded him, ringingly dropping the pin into the shallow rectangular porcelain dish on the marble mantel. "Can't you put it behind you?"

"There is only *so much* I can put behind me." He sassed a finger to his starched lapel. "I'm not Kim Kardashian."

From her bed-corner perch, Janie snorted a laugh.

"Don John," Charlotte continued to pout into the large mirror, loosening her dark, shining tresses under her hand. As they tumbled freely down her perfectly vertical back, Janie blushed. The only thing worse than being ignored, she decided, is *laughing* and being ignored. "Aren't you going to ask about my *meeting*?"

"Duh, I was just gonna!" clucked the young fop. He planted his elbows on his crossed knees, clasped his manicured hands under his chin, and tilted toward her, rapt with interest. "Okay," he ventured. "On a scale of Gap to Gucci — how did it go?"

With a dainty *demi-détourné*, Charlotte disengaged from the mirror and presented her beaming face. "Givenchy!"

"Not *Givenchy*!" He gasped to his feet, plunged a hand into his black Gucci canvas messenger bag, and tossed a fistful of gleaming pale pellets into the air. "You *broke the scale*, you *greedy sow*!"

"Ow!" Charlotte winced as the bone-colored granules hailed down around her head, bounced on her shoulders, and caught in the strands of her hair. "Tell me you did *not* just throw rice at my face."

"Of course not," scoffed Don John, rolling his bulging blue eyes. "I threw *quinoa*, which is *much* higher in protein." He collapsed across the bed, jostling the mattress, and Janie clutched a bedpost, hanging on to her seat. "I knew this day would come," he moaned, burying his face in the voluminous silk bedclothes. "You're off to your big fabulous future as a fashion designer, while I stay behind, waving my Hermès and/or Lanvin handkerchief at the dock . . . just a *person* you once knew. . . ."

"Oh, Juanita, *no* . . ." Charlotte joined him on the bed, smoothing his stormy, highlighted head. Janie slipped off the bed completely, preferring the less crowded floor.

"Who is that mysterious figure in black, they'll whisper," Don John continued his scenario, refusing to be soothed. "Miserable town gossips!" he wailed. "Why can't you leave me *alone*?!"

"Um, you guys?" Janie interrupted. They glanced her way, twin masks of bewilderment, seemingly amazed to see her there at all. "I'm going to . . ."

"No!" Charlotte cried, noticing her hand on the wrought-iron door handle. Don John sat up and gaped in dismay.

"You're *going*?"

"No, I just need to make a phone call," Janie explained, relishing their concern. That they cared whether she left or stayed! It suddenly felt like the highest form of flattery.

"Well, hurry back!" Charlotte chimed, cuing Don John to reswoon across the bed. Janie smiled as the door swung behind her, blocking her view. Not to say she didn't *enjoy* theater, but when it came to *Don John: A Tragedy in Infinite Acts*? Let's just say she preferred to wait in the lobby.

She headed down the hall, ignoring the immaculate Capri Coast–colored walls (not to mention the series of tastefully framed black-and-white portraits of a seminude and fully preggers Georgina Beverwil) in favor of finding her navy Samsung cell, which she unearthed from her disorganized crocheted hobo shoulder bag. Four missed texts! She smiled, eagerly scrolling down the screen.

> From: Amelia
> How did it go?!?!!!!
>
> Fri, 5:58 pm

> From: Amelia
> Btw: Paul says he a VEGAN now!!!! Hahahahahahah!!!!!!! !!!!!!!!!LMAOomg.
>
> Fri, 6:05 pm

From: Mom
Dinner at Charlotte's fine.
Jake will pick up. Call when
ready.

Fri, 6:11 pm

From: Amelia
Just told him his boots are
made of dead cow he took
them off!!!! his feet smel so
bad!!!!!! worse than rotting
dead cowbutt disgusting!!!!

Fri, 6:39 pm

Janie half-smiled, half-frowned, scrolling up to Amelia's second text. Paul Elliot Miller, a vegan? Really? But he, like, *subsisted* on the spicy-style hot dogs from Carney's. The only vegetable she'd ever seen him eat was, like, *relish* (ketchup he considered a fruit). *And* he wore a pin that said "Flesh Eaters." *Then again,* she mused, punching SEND and lifting the phone to her ear, *that's typical Paul.* The boy could do nothing unless it was to the absolute extreme.

"Oh . . ." A male voice filled her ear, and she sipped a breath, glancing to the end of the hall.

Evan Beverwil, in all his board-shorted glory, had just finished mounting the stairs.

"Janie?" burbled a second, excited voice.

"Hey!" She clapped the phone shut and greeted Evan with a strained smile. *Great*. She dropped her phone into her bag and privately condemned herself. *Hanging up on your best friend equals awesome*.

Evan studied the floor and headed toward her, forking his fingers into his thickly tousled gold-flecked hair. Janie focused on the frosty glass of ice in his hand, his softly slapping flip-flops, but then there he was — *right there* — and she no longer knew where to look. He was too tall, too gorgeous, too terrifying — like a tree that had suddenly pushed up through the floor and shattered the roof, cracking all the walls. It took all her remaining willpower to look up. As their eyes met, he swayed an inch closer, almost daring her to step back. She couldn't move. His eyes were too startling, too blue — like sky through a tangle of branches.

"You're um . . . ," he confessed in a low, apologetic voice, glancing toward his left hand, which, she now noticed, gripped a doorknob. "You're kind of blocking the door."

"Oh," she realized, taking a flustered step backward (mental note to self: *die*). Flattening her back against the opposite wall, she drew her eyebrows together, and in a desperately casual tone asked, "Is that your room?"

"Yeah," he admitted, slowly turning the handle, half-hoping

she'd disappear. *There's no way around it,* he acknowledged with quiet horror. Unless he decided to just, like, *stand there,* Janie Farrish was about to see his room: the chamber of lame, the bib crib — *where players took their game to die.* He closed his eyes, trying to make his peace with fate. Not possible. Pushing the door open caused him near-physical pain.

"Omigod!" she gasped, and he braced himself for what was coming — the ultimate four-letter word, the death to every dude's dudeness. *"Cute!"*

"Yeah . . . ," he granted, beckoning her inside and fighting off the sting. "My mom's decorator kind of went ape-shit." He could *still* remember the gleam in Heidi's eye. *Isn't it a wipeout?!* she'd gushed, ushering him inside. *Um, more like a butt wipe,* he'd frowned. The first thing he'd noticed? The knobs on his solid oak bureau had been replaced by *seashells.* It only got worse from there. The entire bedroom had been, like, *surfolested* — from the fringed hula-dancer lamp to the weathered boardwalk floors, from the antique hibiscus-print curtains to the anchor-and-chain "shipwreck chandelier." And then, most shameful of all, the brand-new Al Merrick surfboard mounted on the wall. In another stroke of brilliance, Heidi thought it'd be a good idea to have the board detailed with his name. *Evan* — coming at you in a burst of flame. Man, it was a full-on *tragedy.* He knew dudes — like, *seriously* talented surfers with nothing to spend but the sand in their pockets — who'd *kill* for an Al Merrick board. And here he was . . . using one as a "decorative element."

More like dickorative.

Janie didn't seem to notice though. She wandered over to his built-in bookshelf, picked up a 1940 Ford station-wagon model car, and began playing with the wheels. He plunked down his glass of ice, gently kicked his empty ice-water bong under his desk, and lifted his chin. "That's a woody," he informed her.

She looked up at him and froze. "What?"

"The *car*," he clarified, resisting the impulse to wince. *Awesome,* he thought. *Now, on top of everything else, she thinks I'm a perv.* "That's just what they're called," he explained. " 'Cause the doors are, uh, made out of . . . uh . . ."

No. No *way* was he saying it again.

She laughed weakly, returning the wooden car to the shelf. "It's really cool," she offered, discreetly wiping her hand on her hip.

"I guess." He shrugged, eyeing the petrified starfish glued around his mirror. "It's kind of a surf thing," he added, kicked a foot over his ankle, and leaned against the desk. "Like everything *else* in this stupid room."

"Stupid?" she repeated, darkening those ocean-gray eyes of hers. "Sorry, I — I thought you were all *about* surfing . . ."

"Nah, I am," he assured her. "It's just . . . people tend to latch on to that *one thing* like that's all I'm about, you know? It's like, okay — I love to *surf.* Does that really mean I need white sharks on my *light* switches?"

Janie laughed — a real laugh this time, he was pretty sure — and he grinned. "You know what I *mean*, though?" he beseeched her, loosening up a little. "It's like I can't *escape*."

"Uch . . . ," she groaned, covering her left eye with her hand and watching him with the other. "I feel bad now."

"Why?" He laughed, looming at the foot of his bed. "It's not your fault."

She moved to sit on his bed, then swiftly swayed back, repelled like a magnet, and frowned at her shoe. He noticed she was back to wearing the ones he liked.

The checkerboard Vans.

"So, um . . ." She hesitated, shaking her silky bob. "I actually came up with a few tattoo ideas, like . . . over lunch?"

"You did?" he said, grinning like a total Beavis.

"Yeah, but . . ." She looked up with an apologetic cringe. "They're all surf themed."

"*Oh*." He pushed some air from between his lips, dismissing her concern. "That's cool!" he assured her, plopping on the foot of the bed. The frame creaked, and he bounced up again, inanely dusting off his shirt. "I mean, it's different with a tattoo."

"Really?" she asked, looking doubtful. Before he could respond, she swiveled her bag against her hip and twisted, presenting one side of her long, slender waist. Her black-and-gray dress came together in a crazy row of bright red stitches, like dashes on a map —marking the path to treasure. "Here." She pulled out a marred black sketchbook, flipped it open against her hip, and pointed to the corner of a page. "It's kind of based on this, um, Magritte painting?" She surrendered the book and bit her thumbnail, waiting for his response. *"I don't know,"* she blurted after a 2.8 second-long eternity. "It was just an idea."

He stared down at the book. "It's awesome."

"Oh." She flushed, not quite buying it. "You don't have to . . ."

"No, listen." He looked up, watching her. "I love it." At which point she stopped talking and watched him right back. *You're amazing,* he mentally added, clenching his jaw; for some reason, he imagined jaw clenches assisted telepathy, not that he *believed* in telepathy, but still. *Something* was happening. The color slowly blooming in her cheeks, the near-reflective sheen in her eyes, the barely perceptible heat radiating off her body: a definite conspiracy of signs. Sun streamed in through a crack in the curtain, illuminating the downy hairs around her perfectly curved ear; they were like the microscopic feelers of some glowing, deep-sea creature, something so delicate you barely believed it existed. He clenched his hand and slowly released it. His fingers thrummed like something electric, jolting painfully at the tips. *This was it.*

He *had* to touch her.

"I should have known!" Charlotte cried, bursting into the room. With a start, Evan and Janie turned away from each other and parted, sliding like pads of butter to opposite sides of a pan.

"Melissa just called," the indignant brunette informed the terrified, taller girl, cornering her by the seashell bureau. "And *apparently*, the Pink Party?"

"*Stink* Party!" Don John sang, sailing into the room.

"*Is friends and family only*," Charlotte pushed on, ignoring his quip. "Can you *believe* it?"

"*No*," Janie replied hoarsely, still attempting to recover from the world's craziest spike of adrenaline. She took a deep breath, not quite believing Charlotte wasn't there to bust her. *Not* that there'd been anything to *bust* — well, besides incredibly strange, incomprehensible eye contact with her older brother — *which hadn't meant anything!* she reprimanded the storming butterflies in her stomach. Did they *not* realize? Evan gave *everything* inscrutable come-hither stares. He seriously gave that look to toasters!

"*I know*," Charlotte moaned in sympathy, attributing Janie's fainting effect to her terrible, *terrible* news. "And the only other high-profile event that week?" She paused to milk the horror. "A Save the Whales benefit hosted by *Hayden Panettiere*."

"*Snooze!*" yawned Don John.

"Oh . . . ," Charlotte whimpered, wringing her hands and beginning to pace. "Whatever will we *do*?"

"Well," Janie hesitated, resisting the urge to look at Evan. "If it's friends and family only," she reasoned, "we could *probably* get Jake an invitation. I mean, we're all Melissa's friends, so we're invited. And Jake's my *twin*. I could claim some hysterical codependent we-speak-a-secret-language thing. "

"Yes!" Charlotte brightly cut in, endlessly pleased by the idea. Don John loudly exhaled through his perpetually flared nostrils.

"But how does that *solve* anything?" he asked.

"Oh yeah," Charlotte's delicate face collapsed. "How *does* that solve anything?"

"Well," Janie explained. "He'd be allowed a plus one, right? So *maybe* he could take the celebriteaser as his *date*. You know, like . . . sneak her in under the radar."

"Omigod," Don John clenched his fists by his face and crooned. *"Buh-riiiillllls!"*

"No." Charlotte pursed her lips at the floor. The idea of Jake traipsing around with some beautiful celebrity was *not* sitting well with her. "Not brills."

"Really?" Janie knit her eyebrows into a plaintive knot.

"You're jealous," Don John addressed Charlotte, and then sharply gasped. *"Omigod, you still like him."*

"Oh, Don John!" Charlotte trilled with laughter, making a mental note to revoke his wardrobe and makeup-borrowing privileges — permanently. "No, no. It's just that I don't think it's *realistic*, that's all." Her eyelashes fluttered as she arranged the bright topaz bangle on her wrist. "I mean, *Jake Farrish* going out with a *celebrity*?" Fighting a wave of queasiness, she managed to sniff, "Who'd believe *that*?"

"I don't get it," his sister muttered. "*You* went out with him."

"I have an idea!" Charlotte gasped, giving Janie the brush-off she'd long perfected on panhandlers and Green Peace volunteers. "*Evan* can take her!"

"Uh, excuse me." Her brother planted his elbow on the back of his chair and twisted around. "Do I get a say in this?"

"Are you waterlogged?" she inquired, digging her fists into her dainty hips. "It's a romantic night with a beautiful celebrity."

He tuned her out, floating his eyes toward Janie. "Are you going?"

"Evan!" she groaned, barely giving Janie time to part her Carmex-slathered lips. "Are you honestly suggesting *Janie* should take the celebriteaser as her *date*? They're both *girls*, hel-lo? The whole point is to *attract* attention to the Treater. Not *deflect* it with idle gossip and *queer*-say. And *besides*" — she turned to Janie, oozing concern — "she probably wants to go with her *boyfriend*. No?"

"Oh, um, I . . . ," she stammered, helplessly glancing at Evan. He had his back to her, hulking over his desk. No *way* would he let Janie see his face, which — assuming it reflected the state of his heart — looked like a little shriveled-up widow woman's. *Of course she has a boyfriend,* he thought, feeling his shoulders tense. How had he been so *blind*?

"Exactly," Charlotte cut off Janie's stammering and arced a reproving eyebrow at her brother. "So. Let's be a little sensitive and say you'll do this?"

"Fine," he agreed, inanely flipping through his take-home quiz. "I'll do it. Whatever."

"Vive le frère!" she squealed, ruffling the top of his golden head. "Oh, Janie!" She whirled around with open arms, squeezing her into a girl hug. "I take it back. You're the brilliest brill in Brill-land."

"No," Janie modestly protested, attempting to nonchalantly pry herself out of Charlotte's mosquito clutches. She had a *strangling* desire to explain things to Evan, to tell him she didn't have a boyfriend after all; it had been a silly misunderstanding. At the same time, what made her think Evan even cared? What if she assured him she was single only to have him look at her, like, *Why are you telling me this?* She pretended to focus on Charlotte and Don John — the two of them grasping hands, excitedly jigging in place — and debated what to do. But it was too late. Evan had pushed back his chair; he was getting to his feet; he was heading for the door. *It's cool,* she assured herself. *He doesn't care. He doesn't. Does he? He doesn't.*

And then, the moment before he left, he resolved the issue, lifting his chin in bro-ish salute.

"Later, dude."

Dude? Janie paled in horror. It was the ultimate four-letter word. The *gangrene* to every girl's *girlness.* He might as well have *eviscerated* her stomach, captured the butterflies, and pinned them, wings still fluttering, to the gargling, acid wall. And wasn't this *precisely* why she'd sworn *never* to have a crush on Evan Beverwil? *Not* because it led to butterfly death on a massive scale, but because it led to *total and complete humiliation*? She knew that. She *knew*!

So, if she knew so much, *why* was she standing here, staring after him . . . whipped beyond all redemption?

"Bye!" she chirped softly, raising her hand. But he'd already disappeared down the hall. She lowered her hand and squeezed her arm — hard — and stared at the open door. Why not just say "bye" to her dignity?

Why not say "bye" to her heart?

The Girl: Petra Greene
The Getup: Black cotton hip-bikini by On Gossamer, black light-as-air bralette by Hanky Panky, sterling silver, marcasite, and turquoise rings from Venice Beach, and . . . does pool water count?

"Come on," he begged, wrapping his strong arms around her small, towel-draped waist. The veins tensed at his beautifully wrought wrists, winding toward his elbows like vines. His firm torso, still slick with pool water, dissolved against her back, pulsing warmth throughout her entire body. "Just tell me the code."

She twisted free and pushed him away, escaping to the playhouse's wraparound veranda. By day, the castle-like playhouse belonged to her adopted sisters, six-year-old Isabel and four-year-old Sofia — *but by night.* Petra smiled, too high on anticipation to finish the thought. Paul Elliot Miller, the neighborhood badass with ethereal good looks — like Zac Efron's long-lost, wickedly sarcastic, eyebrow-and-lip-pierced punk-rock brother — was headed straight toward her. They'd been meeting like this for more than a month — well, not *always* like this. In the beginning, the most they did was swim, floating on their backs, gazing up at the star-flecked sky, trading each other's lives like water from glass to glass. Then, after a week of midnights, in the long wavering shadow of the diving board, they kissed — an explosive, primordial kiss that all but pushed them out of the pool and slopped them panting across dry land. Just like that, they just . . . *evolved.*

And there was no turning back.

Petra smiled as Paul hesitantly ducked to avoid the low-hanging, ornately trimmed Victorian roof, his palm flat against the pale pink ceiling. "You know I ain't *never* gonna give it to you . . . ," she teased, and began to walk backward. By "it," of course, she meant Isabel's "top secret" security code, but "it" had a second meaning too — and as far as never giving *that* up, well . . . she was far less confident. "So why do you keep asking?"

"I don't know." Planting his thumb-ringed hands on either side of her naked shoulders, he backed her up against the child-size red door. The veranda's floorboards creaked beneath their damp, bare feet, and he grinned, watching her mouth. "Why do you keep not telling me the code?"

"I told you," she attempted a scolding tone, but his mismatched hazel brown and green-blue eyes conspired against her. "I promised Isabel . . ."

"Oh, *Isabel*," he murmured into her ear, causing her to nearly swoon against the door. The heart-shaped brass knocker dug into her spine. "What's she going to do?" His warm breath caressed her neck. "Put you in the *mush* pot?"

"Sick." She shrugged him off, cupped her hand to the glowing number pad, and hid her pleased grin behind a dripping curtain of butterscotch blond hair. *Ah well,* she thought.

So much for associating mush pots with duck-duck-goose.

"I saw the first letter," her partner in breaking and entering cackled triumphantly as she punched in the code, disabling the alarm. With mock annoyance, she sighed, pushing open the door. The achingly beautiful boy stooped, following her inside. "P . . . ," he pondered, reaching under a ruffled pink floral lampshade. "Wait a sec." A gentle click. A gloating grin. "It's not *Paul*, is it?"

Petra rolled her wide-set tea-green eyes. "Your ego is . . ." Taking in the sight of his now-illuminated naked chest, the damp navy-blue boxers clinging to his narrow hips, she breathed, "Out of control."

He kicked the door shut, and the delicate porcelain teacups on the table rattled brightly in their saucers. Sofia and Isabel always left the tea set arranged and ready in case their dolls, who they believed came alive at night, might be interested in pretend-drinking tea, pretend-eating cake, and pretend-complaining about their busy days. (That's what *they* did, anyway; why should their dolls be any different?) Little did they know it was their big *sister*, not the dolls' own two legs, who relocated their soft, floppy bodies from their respective wooden chairs to the dusty rose cushioned seat by the bay window. And their big sister who used their porcelain cups — leaving them to be discovered in the morning, washed and gleaming in the dish rack. And not *only* their big sister either. Who would have believed it? Gigantic, grown-up Petra, in *their* house, with an even more gigantic *boy*?

"Would you like some *tea*?" he inquired with mock seriousness once she returned to the table, scooted aside the miniature chair, and settled into her seat on the hardwood floor. A half-empty bottle of amber liquid sloshed in his firm grip. His hands — all frayed cuticles, bass-calloused fingers, and chipped metallic-navy nail polish — weren't the type you'd expect to offer tea.

Then again, it wasn't tea he was offering.

"So," Petra paused, watching him fill her tiny teacup to the very brim. They'd spent ninety-nine percent of the time in the pool making out, and, as admittedly blissful as that had been, she was determined to have *some* kind of conversation, you know — just to prove they could. Hooking the teacup's handle with a crooked pinky, she dragged the cup across the table, dipped her flushed face, and boldly lapped a sip. "So," she coughed, tossed her chlorine-saturated hair back, and sniffed. "How was your first day as a vegan? You fall off the wagon yet?"

"Are you kidding?" he exclaimed, plunking the diminished whiskey bottle to the floor. "Turning vegan has only been, like, the best move of my life. Do you even know how annoyed my friends are?" Petra laughed, lifting her teacup to her bee-stung lips. "Seriously," he smirked, shaking his head. "I thought nothing could outdo the time I told them I was a feminist."

"You mean . . ." She lowered her teacup, frowning with concern. "You're not?"

"No, I mean, yeah, I mean . . ." He knocked back his teacup of whiskey without a wince, wiping his mouth with the back of his palm. "*You* know."

"Well, good." She reached to twist her long damp hair into a bun, but her arms were so heavy all of a sudden; she dropped them, falling back on her hands. "I have to admit," she sighed, offering Paul a sloppy grin. "As a smere . . . as a *mere* vegetarian, I'm impressed. I mean, *I* couldn't do it."

"Oh yeah?" he cocked a silver-hoop-pierced eyebrow, allowing the words "do it" to echo between them like a playground taunt. Petra blushed, averting her wide-set tea green eyes. She had a feeling Paul thought she was more experienced than she was, and didn't know how to correct him exactly; that is — not without ruining the moment. And with Paul — with whom every moment was a perfect, encapsulated eternity — "ruining the moment" was fairly high risk. It meant ruining a lifetime. It meant ruining everything.

But she couldn't think about that now. Willing away her worries, she looked up and met his gaze. He crept toward her, blocking the lamplight, his shadow casting over her like a net, and she trembled — caught — waiting to be dragged in.

"Wait . . . ," she exhaled as he traced her collarbone toward her shoulder, a thrill of goose bumps trailing in the wake of his finger. The pattern of freckles across his finely chiseled nose seemed to shift, floating off his face, and she closed her eyes. They were kissing. Hungry, sighing, delicious kisses. Behind her the floor tilted, rose up, and yielded under her weight. She fell into a fog of chlorine, lust, and whiskey-tainted breath.

"*Wait,*" she gasped, wriggling out from under him, and wrested herself into a seated position. From under his mop of lusciously dyed blue-black hair, Paul watched her, confused, but also concerned.

Okay, mostly confused.

"What's wrong?" he ventured, his already husky voice catching in the back of his throat.

Tucking her bare feet under her black cotton underwear—clad butt, she placed her hands on her knees and brooded at the floor. It wasn't the first time he'd asked that question, and every time she chose a new answer, a fresh confession. Tuesday night: *My father's cheating on my mother.* Thursday: *My pill-popping mother's back in rehab.* Friday: *My little sisters are being raised by their nanny.* Night after night, as she bemoaned her sad existence, Paul held and consoled her. "So what?" he'd say. "*You* were raised by your nanny, and you're the sickest girl I know." Or, "It's not your fault your mom's psycho." Or, "Just give me the word, I'll fu—ing curb your old man's face." Maybe it wasn't every girl's idea of romance.

But it was Petra's.

Still, family — problematic though they were — didn't answer his question. *What was wrong* was something else — something she didn't have the courage to tell him.

What was wrong . . . was Paul.

It had only recently felt that way. For the last couple weeks, she'd seriously thought she'd found nirvana or something. It wasn't that she'd *never* made out with guys before, just with the others — Joaquin, Jamal, that one bakery dude, Rocco, in Italy — making out seemed like something she was *supposed* to do, which was to say, she always felt a little removed, as if she was hovering from ten feet above or crouching behind a tree taking notes like Jane Goodall. Not to imply *they'd* pressured *her*. Like a do-it-yourself frat boy, she pressured *herself*, sexually harassing her own mind: Come on! You're *sixteen*. Christina's already had *sex*, and you're getting uptight about a grade-school-level *hookup*? You're cool, and it's a party, and you're stoned, so get over it. Just do it! Yeah, baby! DO IT!!!

Then, one early December night, as a driving rain rattled the real-glass playhouse windows, she peeled off her pool-soaked underwear, shimmying them down to her ankles until they plastered her foot like a damp leaf. Just as Paul leaned in to assist her, she kicked them free — almost kicking his face in the process — and he flinched. She gasped, but then he cracked his eyes open and laughed. And she laughed too. For the first time ever, she was completely naked with a boy, and he was completely naked with her, and they were laughing, and she was just . . . *there*. She didn't have to push herself; she didn't have to hover from a height. Instead, she was *inside* herself, watching *him* — and everything was easy. So easy, in fact, they'd come *this* close to . . .

You know.

And *that's* when she started to freak.

Looking up from the floor, she met his mismatched gaze and swallowed a hard knot of dread. If he liked her, like, *truly* liked her, shouldn't he have asked her out by now? And by out, she didn't mean something cheesy, like dinner and a movie or whatever. She just mean *out*. Like, outside the playhouse. Like, in daylight. Like, in public. It was weird — not feeling comfortable telling anyone about them yet. If what they had was real, then — whatever happened to the real world?

"What is it?" He wrenched her from her thoughts, toying with the silver-hoop piercing on his eyebrow. He was still sitting next to her on the kitchen floor, looking at her, but all she could do was stare at the space between her naked thighs, unable to look back.

"Nothing, it's just . . ." Her voice trembled. *Say it,* she chanted. *Say it.* "Poseur's kind of blowing up," she crumbled. "I don't know."

"Oh . . ." He puckered his mouth in thought, drawing attention to the hairline scar on his full upper lip. "That's what you're thinking about?"

"It's just we might sign a contract," she blurted, attempting to snuff the memory of her cowardice. "And it's a lot more work than I signed up for, you know? Like, this was supposed to be a *class,* okay? Not a *career* choice. And now there's this, like, promotion thing we have to do at Melissa's dad's engagement party. I mean, the dude wears *eight* kinds of fur *per* music video, refers to women as *bitches* and *hos,* raps about *murdering* his ex-wife, *and* he's making everyone who comes to his party? *Wear pink.*"

"Ugh." Paul widened his eyes. "Fascist."

"You don't even know," she continued to lament. "Melissa told me Vivien, her dad's fiancée? Is dying her *pubes* pink." She sniffed with scorn. "What's left of them, anyway."

"So." Paul looked up from his foot and traced a small circle on her inner wrist. "We going?"

"I mean," she continued to rant. "Do you even realize how backward and evil and, and . . ." She halted, registered his question, and blinked, startled. "What?"

He shrugged. "I just think you should go."

"But," she backpedaled. Was he saying what she thought he was saying? In the corner of the window, the crescent moon resembled a glowing chewed-off fingernail. "You . . . you want to go with me?"

"Oh." He hesitated, sucking the piercing in his lower lip. "Yeah, I mean . . . unless you think that'd be . . ."

"No," she interrupted, flushing with pleasure. "I mean . . . no."

"It could be like, anthropological." He looked down, rubbing his hands together. "We'll observe the natives in their natural habitat. You know, like . . ."

She shut him up with a kiss. "What?"

"Nothing," he whispered, pulling her back for another. He wasn't sure why they'd stopped kissing, and he wasn't sure why they'd started up again. But he guessed it had something to do with saying *anthropological*.

As far as words went, it was pretty kickass.

The Girl: Nikki Pellegrini
The Getup: White skinny jeans by J-Brand, bright blue spandex tube top by Baby Phat, bronze leather brass-studded platform sandals by D&G, and spanking brand-new identity by Melissa Moon

"Nicoletta!" Nikki Pellegrini's ancient Italian grandmother, Nikki the First, gripped the stippled white-leather wheel of her metallic gold 1981 Cadillac DeVille, her withered powder-crumbling face contorted with concentration. "Remember," she warned, adjusting her oversize rose-tinted Sophia Lauren sunglasses. "You are my eyes — you are watching the road?"

"Uh-huh." Glancing up from the Sanrio Chococat organizer on her lap (her first official purchase as the Poseur intern), her fourteen-year-old flaxen-haired granddaughter focused on the morning-sunlit palm tree–lined boulevard. In the past four minutes, they'd traveled at most three city blocks, putting their speed at roughly seven miles per hour. Judging by Nonna's ecstatic expression, however, you'd think they were going a hundred seventeen off the edge of the Grand Canyon.

"Stop sign," sighed Nikki.

"What?" Her tiny grandmother craned above the Cadillac's expansive dash and squinted.

"Stop sign," she repeated. "Stop sign *stop*!"

Her grandmother slammed on the brakes, jutting the Cadillac's gigantic chrome grill a good four feet into the busy Beverly Hills intersection. An angry platinum BMW sailed by, horn blaring. "Yes, yes." Nonna shook her head. "He has to honk, so what does he do? He honks."

"Uh-huh," agreed Nikki, returning her cornflower blue eyes to her vinyl planner. With a Paparazzi Pink fingernail pinned to the lower left-hand corner of the page, she dug her pink metallic Nokia phone out of her papier print LeSportsac handbag, flipped it open, and dialed. "Beverly Hills," she chirped, holding the phone horizontally to her mouth and then quickly lifting it to her ear — the way she'd seen Melissa do it. Feeling Nonna's eyes on her, she cleared her throat. "Mariposa Restaurant," she requested, attempting a more professional tone. "Hello, yes, I'd like to make a reservation, please? The name?" She smiled with pride. "Melissa Moon."

Nonna bobbed her painted copper eyebrows. "What kind of name is this? Melissa Moon. Is she a person, or a thing hanging in the sky?"

Nikki raised her hand, indicating her grandmother should wait a moment. "Sorry, what?" she spoke into the phone. "Oh, twelve thirty. Yes. Table for five?"

Narrowing her watery blue eyes and sinking a size five powder blue suede Ferragamo bootie into the gas, Nonna slowly, slowly cranked the wheel. Over the past few weeks, this Melissa

Moon had become the center of her Nikki's universe, replacing all other passions: the boys, the friends, the schoolwork . . . even the MySpace. At first, of course, she had been relieved — not so long ago, her dearest granddaughter had been shunned at school — much like Agostina Maria Bagni, the quiet, long-faced daughter of Pupi, the village goatherd, had been shunned, now many years ago. Agostina was rumored to stuff her pockets with goats' droppings; *if you talk to her,* her classmates had warned, *she will throw them at your face and curse you.* In the end, the only thing Agostina ever threw, *la bambina tragica,* was herself; it was Nonna's young friend, the dashing and wild-haired Innocenzo Spallanzani, who found her, dashed upon the cold, wet rocks in the misty ravine. At the funeral he whisperingly confessed to Nonna that he'd looked into the dead girl's pockets.

They had been filled with rosaries.

If Nicoletta should suffer such a fate, she confided to her friends on the long-distance telephone, dabbing her watery blue eyes with a crumpled Kleenex, *I will not go on. I will not.* After all, *she* was responsible. What was her granddaughter's suffering if not *a message from God*, the inevitable reprisal for Agostina's suicide, a sin in which Nonna and her classmates had played their part? Every morning and night, she prays to Maria to intervene. The sin is *hers*, not little Nikki's. And then, *blessed be the mother of God,* her granddaughter discovers evidence of her innocence in an art project, is exonerated, the Moon girl gives her a job, and she is happy again, full of purpose, and up, *up*.

If only the change had ended there. Unfortunately, in addition to a transformation in Nicoletta's *mood* came a transformation in her *moda*. Or, as her granddaughter liked to put it, her *fashion sense*.

What could be more ridiculous? the old woman pondered, braking for a cat (a green plastic bag) darting across the road. A round of frustrated honks exploded at her rear, followed by a series of whip-whipping cars, drivers glaring out their windows like rabid raccoons. She ignored them, preferring to appraise her granddaughter's current outfit. *If this is what young people call fashion* — she allowed a meditative, arthritic shrug — *then it is the* end *of sense*.

But some say tomato, some say to-*ghetto* — and when it came to the latter pronunciation, Nikki was *all about it*. Gone were the knee-length pleated skirts, matching pastel cashmere sweater sets, and Capezio ballet flats selected with loving authority by her grandmother, and in their place, a pair of white-hot J Brand skinny jeans, a bright blue spandex tube top, and a pair of brass-studded, bronze leather platform sandals. Her customary gold cross, inherited from her late mother, God rest her soul, glinted desperately behind a barricade of gold chain necklaces. Her flaxen blond hair, once accustomed to freshly washed ponies and braids, had been plastered down with Bumble and Bumble Sumo Wax, scraped back into a swirling, braided "side bun" and set with Frédéric Fekkai spray-on hair crystals. Across Nikki's head, like the tracks of a tiny, precise skier, a pale white part zigzagged to her blond hairline. Melissa was contemplating the hairstyle for herself, but before she *committed*, she explained, the look had to be "tasted." "You heard of a royal food taster, right? Well, as Poseur's intern, you get to be our royal *taste* taster. If the look sizzles, *I* get the credit. But if it *fizzles*, girl . . . you got to down that poison by *yourself*. Take one for the Queen, know what I'm sayin'?"

Another girl might have thought Melissa Moon was full-on full of herself. But not Nikki. When everyone in school — including Carly and Juliette, Nikki's very best friends — blamed her for breaking into the Poseur contest, only Melissa withheld judgment, giving her the chance to prove her innocence. And when she *did* prove her innocence, Melissa rewarded her with the most coveted job in school. With the casual ease of a boomerang, everything Nikki had lost — her friends, her moderate popularity, her *life* — came smoothly, serenely sailing back. Before this internship, Nikki had *nothing*. After it, she had everything.

Which was to say, she had Melissa Moon.

"Oh, and if we could get the corner table?" she continued into her tiny cell, snapped open her Juicy Loves Sephora bedazzled heart ring, and rubbed her manicured pinky into the tiny pot of lip gloss. *"Excuse me?"* Her pink gloss-stained pinky levitated under her gaping lower lip. "Uhm . . . did you say *taken* or *bacon*? Because

INTRODUCING

Nikkeesha

KooL!!!*

now with more Ghetto Gold!

* dignity not included

if you said *taken* I'm going to have to tell Melissa Moon — as in the *daughter of Seedy Moon* — that you are unwilling to accommodate her. But if you said *bacon*, I . . . oh, you *did* say bacon? Oh, I'm sorry, in that case she likes it extra crispy. Uh-huh. Okay, then. *Ciao!*"

With a triumphant crack of cinnamon gum, Nikki dropped her phone into her purse and brushed her hands. "Sorry, Nonna," she breathed, settling back into the white leather upholstered seat. "I just had to take care of some . . . *aaaahh!*"

"What?" Alarmed by her granddaughter's sudden scream, the old woman jerked the Cadillac to a halt. "Oh, I can't take it," she panted, clutching her bony, spotted chest. The car lumbered in place, rumbling like a stinking barge. "My heart, Nicoletta. I can't take it."

Nikki slumped even farther into the depths of her white leather–upholstered seat and tried to breathe. Her grandmother had driven straight into the middle of the Showroom, a total violation of Winston law (lower classmen were supposed to be dropped off in the alley behind Locker Jungle). As if that wasn't bad enough, Nonna's Cadillac seriously looked like it ate BMWs for breakfast, i.e., it was *the* most enormous car in the world, i.e., *everyone was looking at them right now.*

"Nonna," she panted, noticing a nearby gaggle of senior girls glance from the car to one another, Chanel glossimer-frosted lips twitching with mirth. "We can't be here."

"We can't be here," her grandmother repeated for her invisible audience. "And yet, *un miracolo!* Here we are." She coughed into her balled fist, then pointed a coral fingernail to her withered cheek. "A kiss, Nicoletta. And then I go."

One kiss and two excruciating seconds later, the mortified girl got out of the car, eyes glued to the pavement, and beelined for Locker Jungle. The Showroom was in full swing, bustling with the usual Monday morning madness, and yet she could still hear her voice . . . slicing through the congestion like vocal Drano.

"Oh, Nikki, dear!"

Leaning against the hood of her cream-colored '69 Jaguar and flanked by her two viperous best friends, Charlotte Beverwil flashed a nuclear smile. In a deep red Abaeté minidress and knee-high taupe faux leather Stella McCartney boots, she brought to mind a long-stemmed hothouse rose. Of course, in the words of the immortal Bret Michaels:

Every rose has its thorn.

"Who *was* that?" the popular brunette pricked, eyeing the retreating Cadillac. "Your *pimp?*"

Laila Pikser and Kate Joliet dissolved into rapturous laughter, clapping their manicured hands to their cawing mouths. Behind her bronzer, Nikki blushed. Every nerve begged her to flee. But *no*, she commanded them. *Stand your ground.* True, she'd *accidentally* kissed Jake Farrish while he and Charlotte were still together. But she'd paid her penance and *enough was enough*. Gritting her teeth, she propelled her bronze metallic platforms toward the Jaguar — an act of bravado that caused Kate and Laila to a) look at each other in numb surprise, and b) sputter a second round of laughter.

Charlotte, however, remained unamused.

"Can I help you?" she snipped as her gorgeous international boyfriend sidled in next to her, folded her into his lavender cashmere-clad arms, and pressed his curving lips to her temple.

"Um, *yes,* actually." The younger girl struggled to keep the tremble out of her voice. "Can you tell me why you haven't rsvp'd to the Poseur power lunch?"

"Um, *yes,* actually." Charlotte mimicked, pursing her lips into a poisonous pink bud. "Because this is the first I've *heard* about it."

"B-b-but . . . ," Nikki stammered, incredulous. "That's impossible. I left you, like, *six* messages."

Charlotte reached into her black patent Chanel shopper and took out her glossy white iPhone. "Hm . . . the only missed calls I have are from Icki Prositutti," she observed, arching her eyebrow like a weapon. Presenting the screen, she added: "And I never take her calls."

Before Nikki could respond, Jake Farrish, in all his grinning, boyish glory, loped up to the Jaguar. He was wearing a faded red-and-black-plaid shirt, old Levis, beat-up black Converse, and his gray United States of Apparel hoodie with the Amnesiac pin; he pretty much wore the same thing every day, which Nikki now realized was a smart thing to do, considering if *she'd* been wearing what *she* pretty much wore every day, he might have recognized her sometime before standing two feet away from her.

"Oh," he croaked in horror, realizing too late who she was. He glanced at his super-hot ex-girlfriend, who'd all but grafted herself into Jules's cavernous man-pit, and pushed his hair into a mussed thatch on top of his head. It was awkward enough dealing with the two of them — but the two of them plus the girl he'd *accidentally* kissed enabling the two of them to *happen*? "Hey . . . ," he laughed weakly, returning his gaze to Nikki, and awkwardly punched the air, "you."

Old Nikki would have fluttered her eyelashes, melting at a cute sophomore's attention. But New Nikki ignored him, to quote her revered mentor, "like a used pair of Spanx."

"Okay." She looked at Charlotte, pursing her Juicy pout. "Then I'll just tell Melissa you're not coming to hear her secret announcement."

"Wait." The older girl stopped her with a haughty tilt of her china-cup chin. Everyone knew "secret announcement" was, like, *the* oldest bluff in the book. And yet. "Fine, I'll come."

"But . . ." Jules peeled off his girlfriend and furrowed his dusky brow. "Today is the one-month anniversary of our first lunchtime together. I thought we would spend it together, no?"

Charlotte fluttered her soot-black eyelashes and smiled, debating how to respond. She *really* didn't want to miss out on the mysterious Poseur lunch. On the other hand, she didn't want to blow off her anniversary, *especially* in front of Jake — who might get the impression her feelings for Jules were *blow-off-able*. Which they *weren't*.

Right?

"It's up to you, but . . ." Nikki cleared her throat, regaining Charlotte's begrudging attention. She'd spent all of seventh grade and most of eighth studying the popular sophomore's every move, and could read her face like a book (except better, because she wasn't *really* into books). When Charlotte was genuinely excited about something — for example, when she first told Laila and Kate her parents had given their permission for her to attend lace-making school in Brugge, or when she informed Adelaide Dallas that her father had ordered a pair of original Manolo Blahnik silk brocade heels (modeled on the ones worn by Kirsten Dunst in *Marie Antoinette*) for her fifteenth birthday — her smile became crooked, and the very tip of her tongue showed between her teeth. But when she was *fake* excited about something — for example, when she'd congratulated Bronwyn Spencer on becoming a merit scholar (an honor Charlotte missed by one math question) — she smiled in this broad, perfectly symmetrical way, and her eyelashes fluttered, exactly as they just had with Jules. If Nikki had even the *smallest* chance of *beginning* to fix things with her fashionably formidable foe, her opening was now. "Melissa *did* say this lunch was mucho importanté." Now she addressed Charlotte's pouting pirate of a boyfriend, widening her cornflower blue eyes. "Maybe the most romantic thing you can do for your anniversary is, like, you know . . . support Charlotte's career?"

The popular sophomore gazed at Nikki with cool contempt. How *dare* she put her in a position where she might actually have to *appreciate* her?

"I see," Jules nodded. If his favorite television series, *Sex and the City* (he owned the six-season DVD set dubbed in Italian) had taught him one thing, it was this: never come between American women and their career. "Perhaps, then, we can reschedule." Tucking a coiling lock of his girlfriend's dark hair behind her fragrant ear, he whispered, "Dinner tonight?"

"Can't," Jake, who was leaning against the Jag's fender, intervened. On his private list of cruel and unusual punishments, listening to Charlotte and Jules plan their "lunchtime anniversary" ranked right around watching porn with his grandmother. But it was all worth it for the opportunity to say:

"We have plans."

"To study," Charlotte quickly clarified, shooting him a dark look. Returning a modified gaze to Jules, she explained. "Ms. McGovern's having one of her epic SAT vocab quizzes."

Jules nodded, attempting a smile. Noticing the disappointment in his face, Charlotte winced with guilt. After all, she knew those vocabulary words backward and forward. And Jules was her *boyfriend.* Her boyfriend who, *unlike Jake,* raced his own yacht off the south of France coast every summer. Her boyfriend who, *unlike Jake,* could tell her she looked ravishing in six languages. Her boyfriend who, *unlike* Jake, would never cheat on her in a hundred, hundert, cento, cent, cem, ciento *years*.

"Forget it," she glanced up at him lovingly. "We'll have dinner."

Jake wheezed out a laugh. Um . . . had she *completely* forgotten this whole "study session" had been *her* idea? That she'd practically *begged* him? *That he'd passed her stupid Ferrari-pants butt-boy the ball?* "I don't know, Char," he warned with a bob of his eyebrows. "I mean . . . do you really want to show up tomorrow not knowing the meaning of *bovinoplasia?*"

Jules narrowed his lion eyes in suspicion. "H'watever you just say is not a h'word."

"Um." He looked scandalized. "*Yes.* It is. *Bovinoplasia* refers to the uncontrollable urge to lean out car windows and yell 'moo!' every time you pass a telephone pole."

As Kate and Laila dissolved into a predictable fit of cackles, Charlotte set her jaw, determined not to smile. It wasn't that she didn't think Jake was funny. That was the problem. Humor was the *one* thing missing in her relationship with Jules, and every time she convinced herself it didn't matter (what her British-Italian boyfriend lacked in wit, he more than made up for in maturity, intellect, compassion, and a Ferrari), Jake would make her laugh, and suddenly all Jules had to offer meant nothing.

To make matters ten sizes worse, he'd started to get a clue.

Like, if she so much as *tittered* at one of Jake's jokes, Jules got all quiet and pensive. Then later, when they were alone, he'd touch her shoulder. "Why is the math book so unhappy?" he once ventured, a hopeful smile on his chiseled face. "Sorry?" she'd replied, baffled. "Why is the math book so unhappy?" he'd repeated as she continued to look perplexed. "Because!" He laughed a little, preparing her for what she was in for. *"It is full of problems."*

Valiantly, she smiled, but it was the same kind of smile her grandfather offered, late in life, after he'd lost his hearing and couldn't follow conversation. A vague smile, like something submerged, trying and failing to show its shape under a shifting surface. And she guessed it was the smile that pushed him to ask, "Are you happy with me?"

She knew what he was really asking: Do you still like me? And she *did*. How could she not with that beautifully sad, worried expression on his face? "Of course," she'd assured him, flooded with tenderness. If only he hadn't believed her! She wouldn't have had to watch the expression disappear. And her tender feeling might have lasted, instead of slowly and secretly ebbing away.

Leaving her with no feeling at all.

"Of course we'll go to dinner," she chimed again, shaking off the memory. Reaching into her black patent Chanel shopper, Charlotte removed a tidy stack of pale pink flash cards bound in silk ribbon from Tiffany's and handed them to Jake. "Sorry I'm bailing," she apologized sincerely. "But . . ."

"Nah." He shook his tousled head and pulled the end of the

ribbon. The pretty bow grew smaller, smaller, and broke apart. "It's cool."

"Those flash cards are pretty much all you need anyway," she assured him, forcing herself to turn toward her devoted boyfriend. When she did, Jules's face melted with gratitude.

She kissed him then. So she wouldn't have to see it.

The Girliatric: Jocelyn Pill Brickman
The Getup: Laguna flared jeans by True Religion, turquoise twill Love Hunt vest by Nanette Lepore, shocking pink Paradiso embroidered slingbacks by Dior, bubblicious boobage by Dr. Robert Greene

Every luxury Beverly Hills department store has a companion restaurant, a place for patrons to check their afternoon purchases, kick up their Sergio Rossi heels, and unwind over conversation, consommé, and credit. At Café SFA, Saks Fifth Avenusiasts indulge in coconut peekytoe crab salad; at Barney Greengrass, Barnistas sample bagels flown in that morning from New York; and finally, at Mariposa, Neiman Marcusites cut filet mignon into bite-size morsels, pinch the pieces between manicured fingertips, and feed them to the quivering purebred dogs stuffed into their oversize Fendi purses.

As far as Beverly Hills department store lunch establishments go, Mariposa's decor met the standard — well, assuming you consider anything in Beverly Hills "standard" (if you attend Winston Prep, fyi: *you do*). The heavy square tables are dressed in the usual crisp white linens and polished white plates and topped with clusters of white and yellow irises. Behind plates of glass, original Calder tapestries decorate the walls — all bold colors and repetitive patterns that can hypnotize, given one looks too long.

No one ever does. At Mariposa, lunching ladies pooh-pooh fine art for something greater: each other. Tossing glances to neighboring tables, they estimate the worth of *that* one's Malibu home versus *that* one's Malaysian nanny, *that* one's anniversary diamond versus *that* one's divorce settlement. They gasp, giggle, gush, and guffaw — until, inevitably, there's nothing left to say. No matter. Widening their navy Dior mascara–encrusted eyes, tilting frosted glasses toward collagen-cushioned mouths, they knock back Prozac with Pinot and smile. Tiffany diamonds melt down their bony knuckles like ice.

Today, however, just as conversation dried up and sugarplum visions of green-and-white capsules danced about their ash blond heads, five young teenage girls sailed into the elegant restaurant, saving them from silence. *At last!* They breathed a collective sigh of relief. *Something new to talk about.* Teenagers were tolerated (albeit begrudgingly) on weekends, but at one p.m. during the *workweek?* Unheard of. And yet here they were, prancing around like they owned the place, crop dusting the tables in noxious clouds of junior fragrance, and dispelling in one glance — in one heady *whiff* — the comforting mass delusion women of a certain type cling to like lifelines.

They hadn't aged a *day* since high school.

"Ladies," Melissa Moon assumed her seat at the head of the table, tucking from sight (to the near audible relief of the Botoxed barracuda behind her) her enviable, high-water booty. With what she considered "regal" patience, she waited for Charlotte and Janie to slide into the plush beige banquette to her left, for Petra to settle into the opposite chair, and her new protégée, Nikki Pellegrini, aka Nikkeesha Kool (in the tradition of Beyoncé's Sasha Fierce, Melissa had encouraged the intern to adopt a bolder, sassier *persona*) to occupy the chair to her immediate right. "I'm sure," Melissa breathed, commencing the speech she'd rehearsed to Emilio Poochie the previous night, "y'all are wondering why, of all restaurants in Beverly Hills, I chose Mariposa to host our first Poseur power lunch."

"Actually," Charlotte tipped toward Petra with an appalled sniff, "I'm wondering why Petra reeks of" — the stale scent of chlorine, Old Spice, and hangover stung her delicate nostrils — *"Disneyland."*

"Get away from me," Petra pushed Charlotte's shoulder and giggled, leaning back in her chair. Charlotte waved a hand in front of her nose.

"My pleasure."

"If you want to know why I chose Mariposa," Melissa boomingly interrupted, thoroughly unamused by her colleagues' *evident* ADD; as the four sets of eyes brightly refocused, she exhaled, posing with her hands on her hips. "I provided a clue in my outfit."

Charlotte, Petra, and Janie perused Melissa's outfit with merry intrigue. Her white Versace stretch-silk dress, cinched into place by a gold Prada butterfly-clasp belt, boasted a pattern of purple butterflies, her Hanae Mori Butterfly–scented earlobes sported pink-and-gold Juicy Couture butterfly studs, and perched upon her smooth, center-parted, raven-haired head, a pair of raspberry plastic Prada butterfly frames shone like a crown. The three older girls shared a surreptitious eye roll.

Either the clue was *butterfly*, or Melissa was in the grip of Mariah Carey mind control.[2]

Tucking the toe of her hot pink patent Doc Marten behind the wooden chair leg, Janie screwed her face up in mock concentration. "Is the clue, butter . . . face?"

"No, no, it's *butterfly*," Nikki corrected her explosively. The three older girls glanced at one another a second time, stifling their smirks. "*Mariposa* means butterfly in Spanish!"

"Fine." Petra tucked her teal bra strap under the torn sleeve of her faded black Bikini Kill t-shirt. (*Since when was Petra into punk?* Janie wondered.) "What do butterflies have to do with Poseur?"

Melissa bitch-slapped the table with both hands, nearly divaporizing an approaching server. "Do you even *remember*," she squawked as the waiter cringingly dropped a basket of freshly baked popovers on the table, "where you people *were* three months ago?"

"Daddy's vineyard?" Charlotte sighed nostalgically.

---

[2] On the *Winston List of High Risk Listening*, Mariah Carey's high notes rank #2 — between #3, *Alvin and the Chipmunks: A Chipmunk Christmas,* and #1, playing "Helter Skelter" backward.

"I don't mean where were you *geographically*," Melissa groaned as the waiter scampered away. "I mean *metaphorically*."

Except for Nikki, who was busy taking the minutes, the Poseur collective regarded their Director of Public Relations with confusion.

"*Caterpillars,*" she sighed, answering her own question. "Except, of course, *worse* than caterpillars. We were *couture*-pillars."

A moment of humble silence.

"*That's* why I decided to hold a lunch here," she explained, pouring a tall glass of Pellegrino. "To remind us of what we were. Of what we *are*. And most importantly . . ."

"What we can become," Janie finished her thought.

With a bob of rigidly gelled eyebrows, Melissa raised her slender water glass. "What we *will* become."

Gripping their own glasses, the colleagues craned across the table. The Pellegrino sparkled and hissed, catapulting into the air the occasional glinting droplet — *like flares on a sinking ship,* Janie mused before retracting the comparison. This was a *toast*, after all, and of all images to have in mind, "sinking ship" wasn't ideal. Still, just before she struck the image from her mind and replaced it with something optimistic (Sasha Obama sliding down a rainbow into a field of four-leaf clover?), the four glasses clinked together. She winced, overcome by superstitious guilt.

She hadn't just cursed them, had she?

As if in response to her question, an ominous shadow angled

across her friends' cheerful faces. "Exactly *what* is going on here?" honked an outraged female voice. Without lowering their glasses, all four girls glanced upward. Jocelyn Pill Brickman — thirty-something ex-wife to studio mogul Bert Brickman, former Miss December and Playmate of the Year and author of the almost bestselling *The Afterwife: You're Divorced (Not Dead!)* — folded her Clarins-slathered arms across the rock formation she called breasts and glared like the world's meanest bus driver. Every Friday, she and her two BFF's, Pepper and Trish, piled into Trish's enormous glossy black Range Rover, rocked out to Jane's Addiction and/or the Beastie Boys, and cougared on down to Neiman Marcus where, after buying fresh sets of lingerie for the upcoming weekend, they gathered at Mariposa to cackle loudly over white Zinfandel and truffle Parmesan French fries. Because yes, *some* things had changed since high school — they'd since traded in cafeterias for cafés and raspberry Crystal Light for Cabernet — but *the rules remained the same.* They were *still* Pepper, Trish, and Joss, the leanest, meanest, homecoming queen-est, I-guess-we-were-just-blessed-with-superior-genes-est bitches around. And, um, *hello.*

"This is our table," aqua-eyed Jocelyn informed them with a toss of her Locklear locks.

"Really?" Petra eyed their intruder's puffed-up piehole in disgust. Nothing grossed her out more than plastic surgery, mostly because it provided scumbag Doctor Daddy with a living. She leaned an elbow on the table, tilting her face at a sarcastically innocent angle. "I thought your kind belonged in caves."

Melissa, Janie, and Charlotte exchanged a look of pure shock. So now Petra not only *dressed* punk rock, but she was also dishing out the snaps? What kind of alternate universe *was* this? From either end of the restaurant, the lunching ladies appeared to share the sentiment, albeit for a different reason: no one had *ever* stood up to Jocelyn Pill, the former Mrs. Brickman.

This was going to be good.

"Excuse me?" piped up Pepper, an aspiring Christian pop singer whose self-proclaimed feisty personality lived up to her name (of course, she kept her *original* name, Mavis, strictly under wraps). "What did you say, you insignificant little *diaper* stain?"

"Forgive my colleague," Charlotte breathed, rescuing Petra from a catfight she was in no way equipped to handle. But before she could follow up with "normally she respects her elders," Trish — a redheaded gym rat with a thing for dating X-Gamers — butted in.

"Colleague?" she guffawed, and hip-bumped Jocelyn. Assuming a singsong baby voice, she asked. "Did we inter-wupt a *meeting?*"

"Wait . . . ," Jocelyn gasped, widening her aqua eyes in awe. "Are you guys *the Baby-sitters Club?*"

As the three women brayed with laughter and gave each other high fives (*High fives?* thought Janie. *Who does that? And what in God's name was the Baby-sitters Club?* thought Nikki), Melissa calmly unzipped her pink Marc Jacobs satchel, extracted a multicolored-on-white Louis Vuitton Murakami card case, and snapped it open.

"Here," she said, pinching out a newly minted pink, black, and gold business card. "I want y'all to keep this. 'Cause you see, next season when our label be blowin' up? And the lines outside Ted Pelligan —"

"*Avec* whom we have an *exclusive* handbag deal," interjected Charlotte.

"Are *around* the *block*?" Melissa resumed. "Y'all can contact me," she advised, slapping the card on the table with the authority of a Las Vegas blackjack dealer, "*to apologize*."

Before Jocelyn could respond, James, Mariposa's manager, who had been alerted by his sensitive staff to the cub-on-cougar tension, burst from the swinging kitchen doors. "Is everything all right?" he inquired, plunking a hot plate of bacon (extra crispy) in front of Melissa and turning to Jocelyn with a placating smile.

"Actually," murmured the buxom blonde, sliding Melissa's card to the table's edge, "everything's fine."

"But . . . !"

"Shut *up*, Pepper," Jocelyn silenced her friend through clenched teeth. Tucking the card into her back pocket, she flashed the manager and girls a bright smile. "So sorry to disturb you!"

The five girls watched Jocelyn and her fake-baked besties retreat from the table, unified by the same thought. *All it took was the name.* At the mere *mention* of Ted Pelligan those women had surrendered — tails between their designer-denim-clad legs. Someday, they incredulously pondered, Poseur could have that same kind of power. As if by magic, tables would open and lines would part, fees would be waived and parking tickets ignored. Someday they wouldn't need Ted Pelligan to make things happen.

They would just *happen.*

"Did I even *order* this?" Melissa suddenly asked, bolting her bacon with a puzzled frown.

Nikki eyed the small plate with a knowing titter.

From the opposite side of the restaurant, Jocelyn began to scowl. *Get your giggles while they're hot, girls,* she seethed, pressing a BlackBerry Touch to her aquamarine-studded ear and fanning herself with Melissa's business card. "Ted Pelligan, please," she breathed, switching her phone to a fresh ear and turning to her friends with a wink. They faced one another and high-fived, barely stifling their squeals. Seemed some fresh meat was about to be fried. And this time?

It wasn't bacon.

The Girl: Miss Paletsky
The Getup: Olive wrinkle-resistant pleated slacks, navy blue pleather pumps, dusty rose stretch-lace turtleneck, and classic navy blazer, all from Loehmann's

At Winston, school ends at three, with the notable exception of Fridays, which end at two. Excluding, perhaps, a *Gossip Girl* episode featuring Nate and Chuck's first kiss (will they get it *over* with, already?), Winstonians could imagine no hour better spent. Which was to say, *what* they did hardly mattered (some gossiped, others shopped, some took their cars to get washed, others flipped through magazines, drawing devil horns on Miley Cyrus); *that they did it at all — that* was the point. They could have been in school right now, and yet . . . they weren't!

Even *flossing* felt like a second lease on life.

Of course, no one — student or faculty — greeted end-of-week early dismissals with deeper gratitude than Miss Paletsky. Her bus commute took about an hour, leaving her just enough time to get home, sigh her Sigh of Unfathomable Woe, and put down her purse before Yuri roared into the apartment, shattering her solitude. Light fixtures quaked, picture frames shifted, tchotchkes jittered: the very *walls* trembled in his presence. No space could contain him. With Yuri inside it, the room creaked like a baby carriage hijacked by a silverback gorilla.

Of course, one might wonder why she rushed home at all.

Why not hole up in her office for a while, or get off the bus one stop early and window-shop on Melrose? Why not kill an hour or two at Sweet Lady Jane, where she could sit with a dog-eared copy of *War and Peace* and a cup of peppermint tea, and where Leon, if he was working, gave her chocolate rugelach for free? As Yuri himself often inquired (albeit when she was running in the opposite direction), *What is ch'urry?*

The answer was simple: she must get home to her piano. Ever since Christopher "Seedy" Moon hired her to play for his pink engagement party, she'd been racked with anxiety. Of course, nerves were not unusual, and under normal circumstances she knew exactly how to cope. Practice, practice, practice. As Ms. Transky had instructed her as a young student: "You must play your pieces until your fingers acquire minds of their own — until your fingers are like your heart. You may command your heart, *stop beating*. Does it stop? So it must be with your fingers. You *must* trust them to play *no matter what*. Only *then* will you relax and play with confidence."

And so, after arranging eight of Christopher's greatest hits into a thirty-minute program for piano, she practiced. "Kimchi Killah," "Death in Venice," "Gimme All Your Love (Gimme All Your Money)," "Little Miss Chang," "Glock to Remember": by the end of three weeks, she knew those pieces like her great-great-great grandmother knew Rasputin (a little *too* well). And yet, despite her preparation, her nerves hadn't gotten better.

They'd gotten worse.

Of course, it *was* possible her anxiety had nothing to do with music. Tomorrow night, after weeks of not seeing him . . . she would see him. And there was nothing she could do — nothing she could *practice* — to prepare. Not that she hadn't tried. She had, according to the age-old tradition of the pathetically crushed out, rehearsed to the bathroom mirror. There wasn't a form of "ch'ello," she hadn't tried: the straightforward, adult *ch'ello*; the surprised and laughing I-didn't-see-you-there *ch'ello*; the wry and ironic *ch'ello*; the subtly flirtatious *ch'ello*; the you're-getting-married-and-I-don't-care-because-my-heart-is-dead *ch'ello* . . .

No, she commanded herself, plunking down at the wooden piano bench with a self-reproving frown. That her nerves had to do with a man she barely knew — an *engaged* man she barely knew — was too mortifying, too *ridiculous*, to consider. She was a grown woman! Not a silly young girl. *Practice.* Her trembling fingers (painted in her signature Krème de la Kremlin) hovered above the keys. *Practice.* The ethereal first notes of "Good Year Pimpin' " filled the air.

And then the front door exploded.

"You make noise like dying bear!" he boomed, rumbling into the room like a Soviet tank. The young teacher dropped her pale hands to her lap and cringed, reluctantly following her barrel-shaped fiancé with her bespectacled eyes. Thudding the short yet well-trampled path from the door to the overstuffed black leather sofa, Yuri reached for the TiVo remote, flopped into his seat, and kicked off his black-and-white Adidas sandals. As the

leather fartingly surrendered to his dense weight, the plasma screen flicked to life, imbuing his already toadlike face with an amphibian green hue.

Miss Paletsky sighed to her feet.

"Where you go?" he grumbled distractedly, not taking his eyes from the TV.

"To the bathroom." What did he want from her? A hall pass?

"Good." He grunted. "Remember to bring me Icy Hot."

With contained exasperation, Miss Paletsky disappeared down the hall. The bathroom, with its flamingo pink sink and toothpaste turquoise tiles, hadn't changed since the '30s, when it hosted the primping rituals of countless aspiring starlets. She tried not to think about them (it chilled her dread), but then: the tea-brown water stain on the ceiling, the hairline cracks along the grout, the sun in the window.

What were they if not a plea to remember?

"Here." She returned from the bathroom and plunked the ancient-looking Icy Hot on the glass table by Yuri's meaty elbow. He grimaced, transfixed by the plasma screen, and fumbled for the three-ounce tube of ointment. Nothing short of a private meeting with President Putin or Carmen Electra could distract him from *The View*.

"Go back to graveyard, Barbara!" he shouted at the TV, unscrewing the tiny cap. "Stewpid peasant."

As he rubbed the ointment into his furry hump of a back, the future Mrs. Grigorovich resumed her place at the piano, wobbly with grief. Not to say she wasn't by now accustomed to practicing with Yuri barking in the background.

But it was Friday.

The day she looked forward to all week.

The day of *the extra hour.*

Did he *have* to take *that* from her *too?*

On top of the upright piano's closed lid, her soap-size plaster bust of Beethoven glowered down at her. Before she quite knew what she was doing, she swiped the sullen composer from his perch, squeezed him hard in her hand, and, with a screech seldom heard outside Kung Fu movies, hurled him against the wall.

"Oigah!" Yuri's arms flew to his face as the tiny statue smashed to smithereens. "You crazy?"

"I need to practice!" she cried, leaping up from the rickety bench.

Still peering through the slats of his fingers, he gaped. *"So?"*

"Alone! Alone! I need to practice *alone.*"

With a dismissive hand gesture, he brushed her off, returning to the television. "Shut up, Whoopie," he muttered, pointing the remote and raising the volume a notch. "Why don't you look for your eyebrows?"

Miss Paletsky stalked across the room, rooted herself in front of the plasma screen, and gritted her teeth.

"Ch'ello!" Yuri raised his arms like a sorcerer conjuring a spell. "I am watching *View*!"

"Yuri," the young teacher declared, "I cannot marry you."

"We talk about this later," he replied, gesturing for her to get out of the way.

"There will be no more talking!" She clenched her fists, stomping her foot. "Engagement is *nyet*."

"*Nyet?!*" Yuri scoffed in indignation. "But you will be sent back to Russia! *Like a dog*."

"Dah, dah!" She clapped her hands once and laughed. "I am dog. I am bear. I don't *care*." Behind her octagon-shaped Lens-Crafters, her brown eyes narrowed. "I would rather be *any* animal in Russia than woman to *you*!"

With a pensive grunt, her scorned suitor gripped the remote and thumbed the mute. "So," he intoned as all around them, silence hummed. "There is someone else?"

Miss Paletsky's brow furrowed with confusion. "*What?*"

"Another man!" Yuri slapped the arm of his chair. "Tell me I am wrong," he challenged.

His fiancée could only laugh, covering her face with her hand.

"*So, I am right!*" He heaved himself out of the black leather chair, knocked into the table, and scattered its contents to the floor. Of *course* he is right! Why else does he come home an hour early, eh? To catch her! To catch her *and* him. But they are too quick! Too clever.

"Tell me!" He gripped his knee, limping forward. Under his naked foot, the toppled tube of Icy Hot gasped, splooging all over the rug. "*Who is this man?*"

"You are crazy," she insisted, shaking her head. "There is no man."

"LIES!" he roared from the opposite side of the room.

"There is no man!" she insisted again, this time bursting into tears. *If only there were another man,* she thought. Yuri sank to the floor and sighed, cradling his cranium in his stubby hands.

He hadn't meant to make her cry.

"Lenochka." He looked up, eyes red with regret.

But she was already out the door.

The concrete hardened under her feet as she ran, stinging her every step. But the pain was a friend — it ran with her — down the sidewalk, past the steady hush of sprinklers and peach bungalow apartments behind water-stained adobe walls, past the woman unloading groceries from her beat-up Saab, past the trio of Orthodox Jews, teenage boys in long black coats, wide-brimmed hats, on their way to services, past the hissing hydrant, the dog behind the chain-link fence, and the fallen palm frond, splayed like a broken fan in the gutter.

Finally, clutching her ribs, she leaned against a rough cinderblock wall and caught her breath. Across the alley, its deep coral pink walls dusky with twilight, the landmark Formosa café appeared to watch her from behind green-and-white-striped awnings. As the half-moon shone through clustered banana trees and valets darted around lumbering cars, a back door swung open, releasing a burst of chatter. Two girls — real shriekers — in skinny jeans, baby-doll blouses, and heels ventured into the night air. *Maybe I'll go inside,* thought Miss Paletsky, watching them dig into their purses. Take a seat at the bar. Have a drink, maybe. Something new — like fuzzy martini. Wait — was that the name? *Nyet.*

Dirty navel?

Minutes later, grinding their cigarettes under their heels, the girls headed back to the bar. There was a second burst of chatter, and then the back door swung shut, leaving Miss Paletsky in silence. She blinked down at her outfit: olive green pleated slacks, navy pleather pumps, dusty rose stretch-lace turtleneck — a scraggly run in the sleeve from snagging her watch — and classic navy blazer. She *liked* this outfit, and yet . . .

A tinny gypsy waltz spiraled thinly into the night air, halting her thoughts. She sighed, digging her cell phone from her hip pocket. The last thing she wanted to do was talk to him, but she must. If she wanted a place to sleep — not to mention a place to wash and dress for tomorrow night — then she would have to make *some* kind of peace. She scowled at the flashing face of her phone, bracing herself for the toxic displeasure that accompanied reading his name. Christopher Duane Moon.

Wait — who?

She frowned at the screen, waiting for the letters to rearrange into the order she expected. They did not. The melody repeated. The name remained the same. She swallowed, lifting the phone to her ear.

"Ch'ello?"

"Miss Paletsky?" a small voice warbled from the other end. The young teacher's frown deepened. He sounded so . . . feminine. "Something *really* bad has happened," the voice went on. "Like, the worst thing *ever*."

Miss Paletsky exhaled, gripping her forehead. "Melissa."

"I know," Christopher Moon's daughter confirmed. "And I swear I wouldn't call you if it wasn't an absolute emergency."

"Where are you?" Miss Paletsky took command of her senses. "Why are you whispering?"

Melissa hesitated. In order to get her Special Studies teacher's personal home number, she'd had to sneak into her dad's office — right next door to his bedroom and strictly off-limits — and nab it from his Rolodex. To make matters ten times trickier, she'd left her damn cell in her bedroom, forcing her to either use her dad's office phone or risk sneaking into the office all over again. Needless to say, Option Office Phone won out, because if she did *not* take care of this situation *as soon as possible* — as in *now* — she might seriously die of a heart attack, which was — uh-uh — *not* okay considering she'd already planned to die *in* her sleep, *in* her nineties, *in* an ivory satin La Perla nightdress, with Marco and/or Pharrell at her side.

Of course, Miss Paletsky didn't need to know that.

"I lost my voice," she whispered, cupping the mouthpiece with her hand. "I always lose my voice in times of severe emotional distress, Miss Paletsky."

"I don't understand." The pretty Russian paced along the sidewalk. "What's going on?"

"He called it off!"

"Who?"

"Ted Pelligan," she whimpered, strangled by the words. "The contract, the celebriteaser. *Everything!"*

"Oh, Melissa," Miss Paletsky fluttered her eyes shut. "I . . ."

"I was like, 'Why?' and he was like, 'Don't insult me,' and I was like, 'What? What do you mean?' and he was, like, 'Ha! Please hold for Mr. Tone,' and I was, like, 'Who's Mr. Tone?' *and he hung up on me."*

"All right, calm down."

"But the party's tomorrow night! Miss Paletsky, you *have* to talk to him. I don't even know what we did!"

"You can't ask your father?" Her eye winked in suspicion. If Melissa couldn't ask her father, then there was probably something a little underhanded going on.

"Daddy's too busy with the party," Melissa replied, neglecting to mention that if her father talked to Ted Pelligan, then he'd find out she'd never canceled the celebriteaser to begin with, and it'd be off with her head — yet *another* way she would *not* allow herself to die.

"I don't know . . ." Her teacher hesitated. She was getting very strong adult-versus-teenager vibes, to borrow a California word, and she wasn't about to play for the wrong team, no matter *how* supportive she was.

"You don't understand," Melissa insisted, gasping every word. "Some fool sabotages my contest, and all the Man in K-Town's got on him is 'seaweed.' Emilio loves the housekeeper more than me. My dad's marrying Vivien Ho. Oh, Miss P!" The letter *P* proved too much for her: Dior-stained tears slalomed down her cheeks; her breath caught in her throat. "Poseur *has* to happen," she squeaked. "It's the only good thing in my life!"

A small smile flickered across Miss Paletsky's face. Against her nobler instincts, Melissa's bratty objection to her father's fiancée filled her with affection. She shook her head, disapproving of herself, and sighed.

"I will see what I can do."

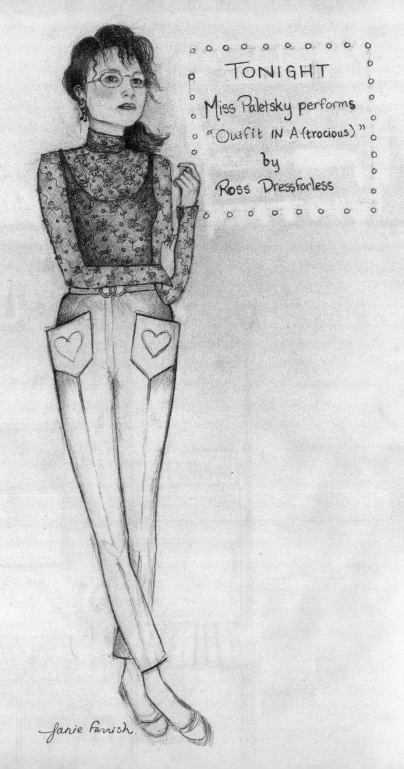

TONIGHT

Miss Paletsky performs
"Outfit IN A (trocious)"
by
Ross Dressforless

Janie Farrish

The Gangsta: Seedy Moon
The Getup: Ed Hardy black tiger knitted velour lounge pants, 18-karat yellow-gold chain by Cartier, carved Korean jade medallion from Momma Moon

Friday night, and Seedy Moon felt like his polished ebony platform bed: *king*-size. Everything was perfect: big half-moon grinning outside his double-paned bedroom windows, daughter tucked into bed, his woman in the bathroom doing woman things . . . no cares in this world. Tomorrow night — with five hundred fine-ass people plus God as his witness — he would formalize their engagement. Had a whole speech planned and everything. "As y'all may know by now, I'm a songwriter. Yeah . . . that means I rhyme for a living. When it comes to settlin' down, lemme tell you — we rhymers be *trippin'*. (Pause for laughter.) Engaged? Rhymes with *caged*. Married? Rhymes with *buried*. Now, with a lot of women you meet — *y'all know who I'm talkin' about!* — those rhymes make perfect *sense*. But then someone like Vee comes along. (Pause to smile at Vee.) You be singin' a different tune. With her on my arm? I'm the *opposite* of buried. With her in my heart? I'm the *opposite* of caged. If y'all want to know the truth (pause to take Vee's hand), I'm walkin' on air. I'm *free*."

Man, every time he even *thought* those words, he got choked up. With shining eyes, he smiled at the closed bathroom door. Was there any finer music than the sound of someone you love taking a shower? The squeak of the tap shutting off, the gargling drain, the shudder of the shower door. The whisper of a towel, the creak of a cabinet, the secret clatters at the sink. For real, dawg . . .

At the same time, he wished he could strip them of privacy completely — broadcast quiet moments like this to the world. Maybe then people would see the side of Vee *he* saw: the tender side, the *real* side, the side he saw the day they met, on the set of *Lord of the Blings*. It had been his first day back to work after his mother died. Pancreatic cancer. Diagnosed, and gone in three months. Needless to say, the whole music-video thing had seemed a little pointless; that is, until Elijah, his director, trotted out a pack of background dancers. There she was — towering over everyone else, violet-eyed, raven-haired, curvy as *duck* — and everything just snapped into focus. Hadn't his mom always been on him to date Korean? Every time he had woman problems: *You no have problem with Korean girl! Korean girl take care of man!* Man, it was annoying. It wasn't like he'd set out *not* to date Korean. Just hadn't worked out that way. The *last* thing he wanted was to turn into one of those dudes who was always like, "Man, you ever been with a black chick? You ever been with a Mexican chick? You ever been with a quarter-Portuguese quarter-Swedish half-Chinese chick?" Like they was trying out ice-cream at 31 Flavors. Like they was ticking off boxes on a *list*.

Gave him the heebie-jeebies.

But then Momma Moon died, and he missed her tiny, junk-yard-dog-mean, disappointed-as-all-hell face so much he couldn't breathe, and — like he said — he looked up and *there she was,* standing by the wind machine, secret smile on her face, shining, wavy dark hair, like some kind of bootylicious Botticelli bombshell, and he just *felt* his momma smiling, like a warm ray of sunshine closing round his neck, and he knew, he just *knew*: she was the one. And he was right. Not only was the woman *hot*, but she was fun and smart, exciting but *chill* — *and* she made him feel like the only brother in the room. Yeah, as he got to know her, she'd kind of revealed a high-*maintenance* side. And she and 'Lissa didn't get along — that was distressin'. But, you know — that was just them learning to share *space* (not to mention *him*), and combine *that* stress with planning this off-the-hook engagement party? There was *bound* to be some tension. Once all the jangle passed and he and Vee sealed the deal at City Hall, the dust would settle and they'd start getting along. They *had* to.

After all, they were the two lights of his life.

"Seedy, baby?"

At the sound of her beckoning voice, he padded his ratty Bugs Bunny slippers across the polished bamboo floor and pushed the heavy oak bathroom door open. A whirling wall of lemon sugar-scented steam parted to reveal his six-foot-tall violet-eyed queen. She stared into the mirror, raven hair swept into a pink towel turban thing, one long, long leg propped on the dark gray marble sink, swirled her polished-red fingertips into a smallish tub of white cream, and dotted dollops on her thigh, knee, calf, and ankle.

"Did you put this on?" she asked, referring to the delicate piano music wafting from the built-in shower speakers.

"Yeah." Seedy grinned, watching her massage the dollops of cream into her perfect, tanned skin. "It's that CD I asked Lena to burn, remember? So I could learn to appreciate classical music . . ." He wrapped his arms around her waist and closed his eyes, breathing in the steamy scent of her shoulders. "Like you."

"Uh-huh," Vivien shrugged, lowering her moisturized left leg to the polished slate floor. "Who's Lena?"

"Who's *Lena*?" Seedy laughed as she lifted her right leg to the sink. "The pianist we hired for the engagement party? Because you insisted on classical music?"

"Oh, yeah." Vivien giggled, dotting her bare leg with more dollops.

"What the heck *is* this dippity-doo?" Seedy grimaced, plunging his finger into the pot of cream.

"*Seedy*." Vivien's jaw dropped in dismay. "That is Crème de la Mer!"

"Crème de la Nair?" he frowned, sniffing his finger. "What?"

Vivien grabbed his hand by the wrist and rubbed the cream off his finger and onto her face. "Do you even know how much this stuff costs?"

"Okay, okay . . . " Seedy chuckled. Hard to take her seriously with shiz on her face. She looked like some crazy crack-lady attempting a Got Milk ad. "How much?"

Clutching the tub to her chest, Vivien narrowed her violet

eyes. "One thousand three hundred and ninety dollars."

The laughter died on Seedy's lips. "Excuse me?"

"And worth every penny," she breathed, massaging the cream into her face and neck.

"You think so, huh?" Seedy snatched the tub from her hand and dartingly escaped into the shower, quickly snapping the door shut.

"Seedy!" His fiancée couldn't help but laugh, smacking the corrugated glass.

"Better be made of pureed *dodo* droppings for that price," his baritone voice echoed as he scrutinized the label. "Let's see . . . okay, *here* we go."

Holding her breath, Vivien creaked open the shower door and lunged for the jar. "Ha-*ha!*" she cackled, taking possession. "You snooze, you lose!"

After a strained pause, Seedy cleared his throat. "You bet."

"You *bet?*" Vivien repeated, mocking the vanilla phrase. And then, noticing the somber expression on his face: "You okay?"

"*Yeah,*" he puckered his brow. "Just . . ." he winced his eyes shut, pushing a thumb and forefinger into the closed lids. "Got a sudden headache, that's all."

"Well, lie down, would you?" Vivien admonished him, kissing him loudly on the cheek. "The last thing I need is you getting sick on our big day."

With a little salute, Seedy exited the bathroom, shuffling his shabby Bugs Bunny slippers toward the ebony platform bed. After so much humidity, the bedroom air kind of chilled. He stretched out on the tautly tucked-in onyx satin coverlet, sank his shaved head into the cool silk pearl gray pillow, and tilted his face toward the row of dark, double-pane windows. Half-moon was still there, but he wasn't smiling. Bed was still king-size, but he was no king. The first ingredient in Crème de la Mer?

Seaweed.

The Girl: Melissa Moon
The Getup: Sheer pink mesh Jewel babydoll chemise with ruffle-lace trim by Cosabella, black silk-satin and pink rhinestone Not Tonight sleeping mask by Mary Green

Melissa was an early riser, but on Saturday mornings, in the name of beauty sleep, she forced herself to stay in bed — not waking until seven thirty, even eight a.m.

The morning of her father's engagement party proved the exception.

All night, she replayed her disastrous phone call with Ted Pelligan in her head — the meeting had gone *perfect*, and it's not like they'd all spoken since then, so then *what*? How in Brand's name had they gone and messed this *up*? When finally, fretfully, she fell asleep, she *dreamed* about it. No answers there either. "Poseur is over," the fashion tyrant intoned, and transitioned into cruel chant. "Poseur . . . oveur . . . Poseur . . . *oveur* . . ." With a whimper, she wrenched awake, swiped away her pink-and-black satin sleeping mask, and whipped aside her sheets, burying Emilio in a 400-thread-count avalanche. It could not have been later than five a.m. (but for patches of moonlight on the ceiling and walls, darkness cloaked the room), and yet she couldn't fathom going back to sleep. Quietly, she slipped out of bed. The blanket mound quaked, and Emilio joined her, tumbling to the floor. *Had calling Miss Paletsky been a total exercise in futility?* Melissa squeezed her hands and began to pace. What on earth made her think a mousy high school teacher in pleated pants and plastic pearls could *possibly* influence the founder of Los Angeles's most fashion-forward store?

Unless the overwhelming scent of drugstore hairspray stunned the man into a state of submission, Miss Paletsky had no chance.

And what about her colleagues? When she called to share the disastrous news, she'd been considerably more pulled together than she'd been with Miss P. "I'll take care of it," she told them breezily. "Just go on like everything's normal and *don't call me*. I'll call you." Ugh. How *confident* she'd sounded. How self-assured!

Melissa curled up on the floor just left of her gold-trimmed champagne princess desk and whimpered in despair. *Nothing left to do but pray*, she realized as her tan-and-white Pomeranian yawned, flopping into the warm crook behind her knees. *But pray for what?*

"Please . . . ," she murmured, fluttering her worried eyes shut. "Just give Miss Paletsky the power to make Mr. Pelligan change his mind."

Ted Pelligan →

and "Debbie"

BeFore the Betrayal

The Gent: Ted Pelligan
The Getup: White calf leather Parigi moccasins by Salvatore Ferragamo, watermelon pink-and-white-striped organic cotton long johns pajama suit from Hanna Andersson

After a day and a half's hesitation, Mr. Gideon Peck quietly suggested to Mr. Pelligan that he come up to the roof garden to rest and relax, and Mr. Pelligan, quick to condemn his assistant's "relentless, *shameless* harassment," nevertheless obliged. He'd spent all of yesterday slumped behind his massive mahogany desk, stabbing his Pimm's Cup with a cucumber spear, and glowering into space; *something* had to be done.

Gideon tucked his superior into a white wicker wheeled chair and creakingly pushed him outside, refusing — despite Teddy's protests — to leave him in the shade. "It might behoove you, sir," he advised, unfolding a pair of green tortoiseshell cat-eye sunglasses and fixing them to the seated man's jowly pink face, "to get a little sun."

"Oh yes," Mr. Pelligan muttered, still clutching his Pimm's on his blanket-covered lap. "Don't you fret, Giddy. I'll be on my very best *behoovior*."

With a concerned sigh, Mr. Peck headed for the ivy-draped exit, leaving Teddy to bitterly resign himself to the "loathsome task" of communing with nature. On either side of the stylish tycoon, purple pansies trembled in their pots. Their delicacy and nervousness annoyed him. He preferred the topiary — hardy little shrubs pruned into pretty, manageable shapes — or the miniature Greek statues — steadfast tributes to beauty, youth, and physical perfection. Contrary to his earlier admonishments, he also preferred the sun — how it warmed his cheek like a Marc Jacobs muff, how it sparkled inside his Pimm's like a Bob Mackie Oscars gown. He never realized it before, but, for a distant ball of burning gas, the sun had *impeccable* style. *Ah,* he mused, settling into his white wicker wheeled chair. *If only it were possible to take yonder Great Star under my wing. To mold that raw talent into something graspable, something grand. Why, under my care, the sun could be fashion's next big thing!*

The idea tickled him, and he chuckled to himself, swirling the ice in his Pimm's — but a moment later the feeling passed. The sun had ducked behind a gathering of clouds, chilling the garden in its absence. *Of course.* The smile withered upon his exfoliated and moisturized lips. *As soon as you put your faith in people, pffft! They disappear.*

Why should the sun be any different?

"Sir?"

"Yes, Giddy," he murmured, not bothering to turn around. A quiet moment passed, and he felt the weight of his assistant's hand on the back of his chair.

"You have a visitor," Mr. Peck informed him in a sympathetic tone.

"I'm afraid I'm like Zac Posen's fall collection, Giddy." He grimly stared ahead. *"Not meant to be seen."*

"A distraction might do you good," his assistant insisted, wheeling him around. At the rooftop's ivy-bordered door, a diminutive brunette dressed in what could only be described as a poly-fester *nightmare* (among its atrocities, the shapeless rhubarb sack included a ruffled chiffon turtleneck, shoulder cutaways, *and* an asymmetrical hemline) offered him a tremulous smile.

"Why is she wearing that?" he whispered, tugging Gideon's sleeve.

"She's on her way to the Pink Party," he replied flatly. *As if* that *made any sense!*

"Ch'ello!" The nightmare moved her painted mouth. "I am Lena Paletsky, Special Studies adviser at Winston Prep."

Noticing Teddy's bewildered expression, the solemn assistant explained. "I believe she mentors the young ladies of Poseur, sir."

"Acch!" The older seated man flinched, then recovered with a glare. "I told you *never* to say that word," he trembled. "Impale my ear with this *cucumber* spear, why don't you?"

"Please, excuse him." Mr. Peck returned to the peculiar-looking visitor and apologized. "He and, er . . . the *girls* had a bit of a falling out."

"A falling out?" Teddy scoffed, fishing an ice cube from his cup and pressing it to his nearly nonexistent throat. *"That's* what you call the most traitorous event since the age of Benetton Argyle?"

"Benedict Arnold, sir," Giddy corrected him.

"Those pretty little turncoats were seen lunching at Neiman Marcus!" He quaked, pitching the ice cube into the manicured grass under his small white-moccasin-clad feet. Miss Paletsky, who hadn't yet worked up the nerve to venture from the doorway, flinched, and Mr. Peck sighed, surrendering himself to the inevitable. Every two hours or so since the incident, Teddy launched into the same speech, speaking as though his words had just sprung to mind and his listeners had yet to hear them.

"Long ago," Mr. Pelligan addressed Miss Paletsky, "Neiman Marcus was chaired by Stanley Marcus, my very closest friend . . . *at the time.*"

"They met at the annual League of Moguls conference," Mr. Peck explained.

"We had so much in common!" he declared. "Both heads of elite department stores, both Harvard men."

"Of course, Mr. Marcus actually attended the university," his assistant reminded him.

"Yes!" Teddy sighed. "He always was so *conventional.* In any event," he returned to Miss Paletsky. "Stannie invited me to New Mexico where he and his wife — *horrible* woman — shared an estate. He was an avid art collector, and *obsessed* with these primitive statues, religious *icons*, if you will, sold by *ghastly* National Geographic types in their dusty *pueblos.* Stanley bought their baubles for a few dollars, a bead necklace perhaps . . . and years later they appreciated *tens of thousands of dollars.*"

"The most valuable of all was the Holy Child of Atocha," Gideon, who had by this time committed Teddy's wearisome tale to memory, cut to the chase. "Atocha, if you're fortunate enough *not* to know, is the patron saint of travelers who risk capture by non-Christian enemies."

"The last time I saw Stannie," Mr. Pelligan, too swept up in the memory to acknowledge Gideon's impudence, pressed on. "He was very sick. Every night, he took Saint Atocha to bed like a doll. 'My most cherished little statue,' he told me with a smile, reaching for my hand. 'I leave to you. Teddy Pelligan. My most cherished of friends.' " He removed his cat-eye sunglasses and frowned, pinching the bridge of his small, bulbous nose. "And can you guess," he sighed, "who he left it to, in the end?"

From the door, Miss Paletsky glanced at Gideon, betraying her utter loss.

"HE LEFT IT TO ELTON JOHN!" the small man erupted, clutching the arms of his white wicker chair and rocking in his seat (the passage of time did little to quell the pain). "That tiny dancer," he spewed in contempt. "That *rocket* man!"

"It was quite the scandal," Giddy admitted, and then — unknowingly explaining why Jocelyn Pill-Brickman recalled the incident while the Poseur girls did not — "in 1991."

Miss Paletsky gaped between the two men in absolute befuddlement. "And this . . . ," she paused, attempting to wrap her mind around it, "*this* is why you refuse to work with the girls? I don't understand. What do they ch'ave to do with this?"

Gideon sighed. He sympathized with her confusion — it was all so ridiculous — and yet, he was an assistant — a good one, if solemn — and understood his duty. "They were seen eating at

Mariposa . . . *the Neiman Marcus restaurant*."

"The very same as spitting in my face!" Teddy sputtered, spitting into the air.

"I don't believe it," Miss Paletksy murmured after a pause, frowning at her feet. There was a word for this. Once, when Yuri was watching *View*, Barbara told Elizabeth this word. "Petty," she remembered quietly, looked up, and found Mr. Pelligan's pale gray eyes. In a strong voice, she declared, "You are being petty!"

"What did she say?" Mr. Pelligan elbowed Giddy in the hip. The assistant cleared his throat, resisting a smile.

"She believes you are being *petty*, sir."

"My dear woman!" he guffawed in shock, jiggling the ice in his glass. "I have been called many things. Delusional. Bipolar. Machiavellian. Homosexual. But, *petty*!"

"But this is *true*," she insisted, abandoning the ivy-bordered doorway at last and venturing boldly onto the landscaped roof. "You want to ch'ave *real* problem? My parents — dead. I ch'ave no one. And because I refuse to marry man who eats toenails? *Oigah!*" In his seat, the well-preserved man cowered. "Back to Russia," she cried. "Cold, miserable, Land of No Opportunity *Russia*. Where streets are not paved in gold, but *regular asphalt*."

"You can't go back!" Birdie, who'd been eavesdropping from the fire escape, suddenly wailed, her right eye lolling to the sky.

"But I can," Miss Paletsky — who didn't have the time to be startled — contradicted, resolute. Mr. Pelligan watched the Russian teacher with wide eyes as she slowly approached him. "And you want to know why?" she asked, gazing down with the fierceness of Atocha himself. "Because at least I accomplish something. So, I cannot ch'ave American dream. At least I bring together four girls who can."

Young Birdie clasped her hands.

"Please," the young teacher continued, softening her tone. "Put this silly grudge behind you. Do not be like Elizabeth Hasselbeck."

Ted Pelligan leaned back in his seat, his gray eyes still wide with wonder. Everyone waited: Gideon with his slender hand on the back of his chair, his daughter, still brimming at the fire escape, and *the visitor*, watchful behind her octagon eyewear.

"To be perfectly frank," he replied hoarsely, pausing to clear his throat. "I haven't heard a word you've said."

Birdie covered her face. Gideon gasped. "Sir!"

"You're surprised?" He craned his round neck to squint up at his assistant. "I'm supposed to listen with that tremendously loud outfit of hers *caterwauling* at me like a cat in heat?"

"I understand," Miss Paletsky surrendered, nodding. "You ch'ave said no."

"Yes, yes, for *now*," he replied, tugging again at his assistant's starched sleeve. "Giddy," he instructed, "take this poor woman into my store, give her a blowout, find her a dress — something that won't devastate my eardrums — and then return her here."

"But," the young teacher began to fret, "I can't . . ."

"If she *must* wear pink," Mr. Pelligan blithely ignored her, instructing Gideon, "then . . . *ah!* The strapless Charles Chang Lima with the lovely little pleats and sweetheart neckline. Yes, that will work wonders for her. With the fuchsia lizard-embossed platform Dior pumps, don't forget. And chisel off that kabuki paint while you're at it. Make her up in something subtle. Chanel Luminous Satin Lip Color in Darling should do. Or perhaps Voluptuous. Oh, try them both and see what works. Use your *judgment*, Giddy. Maybe then I'll know what she's blabbing on about."

"You don't understand," the increasingly anxious Miss Paletsky seized her window. "I cannot afford . . ."

"No, no, I can't *hear* you!" Mr. Pelligan interrupted, cupping his hand to his ear. Only then did she catch the merry light in his eyes. Only then did she know.

It was on him.

"Now go change your dress before I go deaf!" he blustered, fishing another ice cube from his tumbler of Pimm's.

Giddy offered his arm with a gallant smile.

The Girl: Janie Farrish
The Getup: To be determined . . .

In addition to sunshine, Ted Pelligan's rooftop garden provided spectacular views of the Hollywood Hills. From a distance, the winding canyon roads appeared veinlike or invisible, hidden as they were behind eruptive plant-life; sprawling cliff-side homes were no larger than birdhouses, their daunting gates and wall-to-wall windows reduced to dewlike glints. One of these birdhouses belonged to the Beverwils, one of those glints to Charlotte's bedroom window, and behind that glint, microscopic as a speck of dust, Janie Farrish regarded her reflection in an ornately gilded, full-length mirror. From *her* perspective, of course, the Beverwil Estate was more than lifesize — it was larger than life — and Ted Pelligan's rooftop was the negligible smudge, just one of thousands in the broad city landscape below.

"What do you think?" she asked in a hesitating voice, shaking the pink gossamer skirt of one of eight cocktail affairs Charlotte suggested she try on. The dresses belonged to Georgina Malta, Charlotte's knockout of a mother, who (if little else) shared Janie's willowy, slender build. Most of the dresses were two, three decades old, relics of her Paris runway days, "wearable memories," she'd sigh, pressing a deep red velvet hanger to her collarbone, smoothing the dangling gown against her waist, and gazing into the mirror. Around the time Charlotte turned fourteen, Georgina gave her permission to borrow them: "Whenever you like, darling." Yeah, right. Charlotte was *far* too runty to wear those clothes, and her two-faced mother knew it; her generosity somehow *required* it — always extended to those bound to say no.

She once fixed a salad for the cat.

C'est la vie. Charlotte made do with what meager pleasures there were to be had dressing Janie, who, as it happened, was waiting on her all-important opinion.

"I don't know . . ." she trailed off, reclining into her mint green velvet chaise longue and wrinkling her nose. Janie glanced back at her reflection and hoped her warming cheeks wouldn't betray her wounded pride (Charlotte's "I don't know" carried all the punch and sting of "You look hideous"). The dress, a foamy confection of polka-dotted petal pink chiffon, gathered at the waist and held up by whispery halter straps, was gorgeous. More than gorgeous: it was *Valentino*. If Charlotte had a problem, Janie decided, it wasn't the dress.

It was her in it.

"Dojo?" piped the pretty piranha, fluffing the ruffled tulle of her new pale pink-and-black slip. "What do *you* think?"

Don John, busy pressing Charlotte's choice for the evening — a rather modest belted Madonne dress by Dior — turned toward Janie and sighed, momentarily dispersing a cloud of vapor. With his handheld steamer, gelled streaky-blond pompadour, and exaggeratedly bored expression, he resembled the caterpillar in *Alice in Wonderland*. Of course, Janie hardly imagined Lewis Carroll's caterpillar wore Elizabeth Arden bronzer and MARC by Marc Jacobs heart flip-flops. She also doubted he said things like . . .

"Oh, please. Can we say Valenti . . . *no*?"

"Fine," she laughed in defeat, impressed by his seemingly endless store of shock and outrage. She also laughed because she was beginning to like him (unlike *some* people, he seemed to blame the badness on the *dress*, not her) and wanted him to like her too. "I'll take it off." She schlumped off to the bathroom to change. Even though Janie envied girls who could strip down in a locker room and keep talking to their friends like their boobs weren't, you know, *right there* (and isn't that the curse of the flat-chested? It's impossible to act like your boobs aren't "right there" when they really *aren't*?), she wasn't about to pretend she was one of them. Which brings us to the second reason she liked Don John: he gave her a good excuse to change in private.

He *was* a boy, after all.

"Ooo . . . try on the Escada!" his Texas twang enthusiastically commanded from behind the cracked bathroom door. "That thing is so eighties, it makes its own Michael Jackson noises."

"Omigod, I *know*," Janie cackled in delight. A minute later, she bounded outside in a beaded fuchsia shoulder-padded sheath.

"Check. It. Out."

"Oh honey . . . " Don John clapped his hand to his mouth and briskly shook his head. "How many Corys were killed to make that dress?"

"It's nice to see you two still have your sense of humor,"

Charlotte scowled, flouncing from her velvet seat as the two collapsed into giggles. "Considering we're in a *crisis*."

At that, the tittering duo fell into cowed silence. Dressing up had been so fun they'd forgotten all about the Ted Pelligan debacle. Last night, Nikki set up an emergency conference call, and Melissa broke the devastating news. Pelligan was out — no contract, no celebriteaser, and — adding insult to injury — no explanation. *But,* their Director of Public Relations had assured them, *she was on the case.* Obviously, there'd been some kind of misunderstanding. All she had to do was get to the bottom of it to build them back up to the top. Janie, who'd been waiting to hang up the phone so she could dissolve in a flood of tears, had taken a breath, instantly fortified. If Melissa could sound so calm and confident, then things *definitely* weren't as bad as they sounded.

Unless she'd been bluffing?

"Maybe we should call Melissa," Janie blurted, a flutter of panic returning to her heart.

"No . . ." Charlotte frowned, smoothed her frothy slip, and floated like a blossom across her polished maple-and-walnut-checkered floor. "She said she'd call us, remember?"

"But it's already three forty," Janie noted as, with the efficiency of an army general, Charlotte scanned her marbled-topped Art Nouveau vanity and, from the artfully arranged assortment of gleaming perfumes, plucked an amber bottle of Serge Lutens A La Nuit. She *really* wasn't one to brood on a crisis — she'd only mentioned *the debacle* to disrupt the disconcerting bond brewing between her two friends (would they discover they had more in common with each other than they did with her? The idea bruised Charlotte's heart). But now, with Don John's focus returned to steaming her heavy crepe dress and Janie's returned to her, she felt she could return to the subject at hand.

"You're not *really* going to wear that, are you?" she frowned, eyeing Janie's glittering sheath. "You look like the Ghost of Miss Americas Past."

"Um, exactly!" Don John implored the dainty damsel. "Could she be more *faboosh*?"

"It *is* pretty hilarious," Janie hesitatingly smiled.

"*Janie.*" The petite brunette arched an ebony eyebrow. "You want this boy to think about sleeping with you. Not putting you to sleep."

"Boy?" young Don John perked up like a nipple in January. "*What* boy?"

"Oh," Janie stammered, searching for a way out of the subject. "I . . ."

"His name is Paul," Charlotte informed him. "He's in a band, and *apparently* . . ." Janie watched in horror as she skipped to the open MacBook on her bed, clattered a few keys, and brought up the Creatures of Habit website. "*He*"— she grinned, triumphantly pointing to the screen — "is into Janie."

"'Paul Elliott Miller . . . ,'" Don John read out loud as Janie, mortified, darted back into the bathroom. "Lovin' those L's, Lady Farrish!" he called after her. "La la *love* them."

"I'm not going with him, actually!" Janie informed them, feeling braver behind the bathroom door. "We, um, broke up."

"Oh no . . . ," she could hear him groan in contempt, closing the laptop. "La la *loser!*"

Quickly, Janie shimmied free of the sheath, tripping in the fabric gathered at her feet. The silence on the other side of the door worried her. She didn't want them whispering about how tragic and pitiful she was. Or worse, suspecting she'd invented the date to begin with.

"Look!" She laughed, waving her hand even though no one could see her, and her laughter echoed back, mocking her. "It's not a big deal."

"But now you're going alone," Charlotte reminded her — and Janie detected a *trace* of smugness.

"I'm taking Jake," she shot back, scowling at the closed door. Clearly, it wasn't the coolest thing to take your brother as a date, but at least her brother happened to be Charlotte's ex-boyfriend.

"Dress is pressed!" Don John eyed his handiwork as Janie emerged from the bathroom in a sexy midthigh-length coral-pink Alaïa stretch dress. He looked up and instantly stepped back, gazing at her in approval. *"Hot."*

She turned, attempting to study the mirror and at the same time avoid Charlotte's reflected green-eyed gaze. "Really?"

"And a *half,*" he assured her, gently surrendering the crisp Dior frock to Charlotte. "Next time?" He eyed Janie a second time, brushing his hands. "I'm using *you* to steam that dress."

The petite brunette bit her lower lip.

"I'm not wearing this," she blurted, pushing the dress back into Don John's arms.

"What?" Don John gaped between her and the impeccably pressed fruits of his labor. "What do you want me to *do*? Inject it with Botox?"

"Hilaires," she breathed, disappeared into her walk-in closet, and emerged moments later with a candy-pink strapless jacquard dress. "Now," she asked, holding it up like a freshly caught trout. "What do we think of this?"

The dress, strapless, slinky, was infinitely sexier than the Dior — but hadn't Charlotte been dead set *against* sexy? ("I want classy," she'd insisted. "Not assy.") So, what had happened in the last two minutes to make her flip?

Don John and Janie shared a glance.

"Just out of curiosity," the Valley girl ventured, fairly sure of the answer. "Why'd you change your mind?"

The question had barely left Janie's lips when Charlotte's cell phone rang. *Merci bien,* she breathed, dissolving with relief. But then she read the caller ID. "It's Melissa," she gulped, clutching her white iPhone like a cross and catching Janie's eye. All this time, they realized, the drama of dress-up had been a distraction. Now the moment of reckoning had arrived, and their hearts were spiked with dread. No, that wasn't right. The dread had been there the entire time; they'd merely managed to look *past* it, like you do with spots on a mirror. But the ringing phone shifted their focus, and now — spots were all they saw. What if the celebriteaser really did fall through? What if, despite her repeated assurances, Melissa couldn't just "fix this"?

What if they were dressing up for nothing?

"Hey," Charlotte answered the phone as Janie ravaged an already severely handicapped thumbnail. "Okay. Okay. Right. Yes, I'll let him know. Bye."

With a heavy sigh, she clapped her cell shut and resettled into the chaise longue.

"All right, bitch," her Texan sidekick clucked after a full beat of silence. "The suspense thing is getting old."

"Please?" Janie added. "I'm seriously dying."

"Good," Charlotte replied, cool as a cucumber face mask. Janie's lower lip trembled.

"Isn't what happened bad enough?" she warbled, feeling a little unhinged. "Do you have to be so . . ."

"*Gabrielle* Good," Charlotte interrupted, melting into a radiant grin.

Janie crumpled her brow, utterly confused. "What?"

"By Jonas, I think I've got it," Don John realized out loud. "Gabrielle Good is your celebriteaser?"

"*What?*" Janie gasped. "How is that possible? What about the contract?"

"Back on the table, bébé!" Charlotte laughed, clapping her small hands. "Melissa totally got Miss Paletsky to talk to Mr. Pelligan, and apparently it *was* all a misunderstanding!"

"But *what* was the misunderstanding?!" Janie sputtered.

"Melissa said she'd explain later, and besides, Janie, who cares? I swear, your obsession with every little *detail* is seriously, like, *autistic*."

"Just because I'm *curious*," the slender, tall girl bravely defended herself. "Doesn't mean . . ."

"Shh." Charlotte serenely glided to her bed and pried her laptop open. "I have to Skype Evan."

"Isn't he, like, next door?" Don John reminded her, crowding her at the computer. Janie melted to the floor. Not to imply she'd *forgotten*, exactly — she could practically *feel* Evan's presence pulsing through the walls.

"He's at Joaquin's," Charlotte replied, lightly clacking the keys.

Janie flushed. *Oh.*

And then he appeared on screen — not that she could see him through the Charlotte–Don John fortress.

"You're going on a date with Gabrielle Good!" his sister burbled, clapping her hands at the pristine white screen.

"Who?" the laconic surfer replied, decidedly unenthused.

"You know," she groaned, rolling her greenish blue eyes. "She's on that reality show, *The Good Life*? Garrett R. Good's illegitimate daughter?"

"Illegitimate then adopted," clarified Don John, shouldering Charlotte aside and hogging the Evan-filled screen. "She used to be kinda fug. But then she got all waify and fab, you know, with the hipbones and the bug glasses and the Starbucks? She's totally, like, this fashion icon now."

"Uch!" Charlotte pushed him aside and resumed her place, smacking the feather-topped mattress (she could *see* Evan had no idea who they were talking about). "Ev-van . . . ," she enunciated, "the blond girl in that one SNL video. Remember? The one who spanked Andy Samberg?"

"Oh *yeah* . . ." Her older brother smiled, his memory success-fully jogged. "She's hot."

Janie fluttered her gray eyes shut. *It's nothing,* she reminded herself. He'd already diced up her heart and skewered it like chicken satay. "Hot," was just like . . . the dipping sauce.

"She's at the Mondrian," Charlotte went on, referring to the sleek, trendy hotel on Sunset. "You're supposed to pick her up at eight."

"Word."

Charlotte closed her laptop with a snap.

The Guy: Jake Farrish
The Getup: Um . . . more like the upchuck

Charlotte devoted an entire floor-to-ceiling mahogany bookcase to her cherished fashion magazine collection — organized in alphabetical order by month — and from these hallowed shelves discovered one *Nylon*, one *W*, and two *Teen Vogues* with Gabrielle Good on the cover (of course, the reality starlet dominated countless copies of *Us* and *People*, but Charlotte deemed those publications "too common" for permanent library placement). With Don John departed for acting class, she and Janie dressed, and Jules and Jake not due to pick them up for another two hours, there was nothing else to do but pore over every page, scrutinize each photograph, and to her delight (and Janie's private horror), pronounce Miss Good "gorgeous" in every single one. "She's so perfect for the Treater I could scream," Charlotte remarked in a tone meant to convey she'd never be so uncool as to scream: it was just an expression. After all, she wasn't exactly in awe of Gabrielle Good — merely grateful that other, potential Treater-buyers were. "She could carry a bucket and people would snap them up like Birkins," she sighed. Janie had no choice but to agree. To do otherwise would look like lack of support for Poseur, or worse, jealousy, and it'd take Charlotte two seconds to put together why. And then God knows what humiliations she'd endure.

"Don't you just *love* her emerald eyeliner?" Charlotte pointed her Pink Satin polished finger to a photograph. Of course, *she* would have restricted the liner to the upper lid only. Around the *entire* eye was a little vulgar.

"Yeah," Janie murmured, as if the eyeliner mattered, and not the brown eye itself, alive with a sparkle that said "I'm fun, fearless, and seriously *not* a virgin." She wanted nothing more than to stab that sparkle with a sharp object — Charlotte's antique ivory-and-gold chopstick hair ornament would do — and two hours of resisting the impulse completely wore Janie out. By the time Jake rumbled up in their black Volvo sedan, she almost whimpered with gratitude. *At last! For at least one car ride, I can relax.*

But, of course, she was wrong.

"You are *not* wearing that!" she gasped as soon as she carefully placed herself in the car seat.

"Um, okay," he agreed, just to piss her off. The Beverwils' combed gravel drive crunched under their wheels as they pulled through the automatic wrought-iron gates and turned onto Mulholland Drive. Predictably, her brother sat up, both hands gripping the wheel. Most of the time on the road he spent slumped into his seat, one hand on twelve o'clock, and nodding mindlessly to the radio. But Janie saw through his Wu-Tang ways. Every time they got on a canyon road at night he'd freak out, straighten up in his seat, and drive like Grandma Firestein. Under normal circumstances, she found this endearing.

But *normal* no longer applied.

"Is there something wrong with you?" she sputtered, still gaping at his outfit. "The invitation said to wear *pink*, not *crazy*."

"Uh, sorry," he scoffed, easing on the brake. "But if I actually spent money on an all-pink clown suit for a Pink Party — something that's bound to happen *never again in my lifetime* — *then* I'd be crazy."

"*I* spent nothing," Janie pointed out with a lift of her eyebrows. "Okay? You can spend nothing without reducing yourself to mom's *tracksuit*." Against her better judgment, she eyed the offending outfit a second time. Of course, the pink terry tracksuit was about five sizes too small, halting above her brother's inevitably hairy-guy ankles, straining across his broad yet skinny chest, and inching above his narrow waistline. God, he was so *gross*.

"Stop!" he mock whined, hiding his profile behind his raised shoulder. "You're undressing me with your eyes!"

"I'm strangling you with my eyes," she snapped back.

"Come on." He lowered his shoulder and defended his choice. "It's Juicy Couture."

"It's GAP, Jake." She narrowed her eyes. "It says so in huge white letters on your ass."

"Well, whatever the label," he lisped in a motherly falsetto. "It's *extremely* comfortable, I mean . . . the fabric really *breathes*."

"I totally hate you," Janie grumbled, gazing out the window at the night sky and shadowy, hulking hills. They were on the freeway now. High above, the stars glittered, but rather than surrender to their magic, she was reminded again of Gabrielle Good. The *Nylon* issue featured this totally obnoxious photo spread of her traipsing around Venice Beach, spaghetti strap slipping off her shoulder, blond hair cascading to her waist, a quote in bold orange font: I'M MORE OF A "DO FIRST, THINK LATER" KIND OF GIRL. *Ucchh* . . . Janie unconsciously glared at a blue Toyota in the neighboring lane. *Do* what *first, exactly?*

Behind the Toyota's backseat window, an androgynous Goth kid bugged out his or her liquid-eyelinered eyes and sarcastically waved. Janie snapped from her stupor and blushed, averting her eyes. Not that she'd needed to; Jake was switching lanes. In seconds, they'd coasted down the off-ramp, and he carefully began to turn right, inching ahead to the tick of his blinker.

"What do you think of Gabrielle Good?" Janie ventured once the Volvo groaned onto Sunset. "Do you think she's pretty?"

"That's Bellagio, right?" Jake tapped the brake and stopped at the red light. To their left, at the end of a short drive, stretched a giant wrought-iron gate flanked on either side by moon white Spanish arches. Tucked into recessed plinths, pruned potted ivy plants sat like icons in a church. Above the gate, propped into place by ornate wrought-iron swirls, a lantern glowed. The traffic light switched green, and Jake eased into the intersection, waited for a black Bentley to pass, and turned left. As they rolled past the arches and under the gate, a pale light swept through the car.

They'd officially entered Bel Air.

"I don't know. . ." Janie gazed at the slowly passing estates — each more spectacular than the last — and bitterly imagined Evan carrying Gabrielle, his beautiful new bride, across *that* threshold, then *that* threshold. "I *guess* she's pretty." She scowled as the disgustingly in-love newlyweds paused beneath a blooming arbor to kiss. "In an *obvious* sort of way."

"*Man*, Charlotte looked good," Jake remarked out of nowhere, recalling the sight of his ex-girlfriend getting into Jules's Ferrari: her long legs, her perfect ass. "It's like" — he clenched the wheel, quaking a bit in his cracked-vinyl seat — "you know?"

"But isn't she, like, *twenty-one?*" Janie folded her long arms across her tightly bound chest and scoffed. Jake shook his tousled head and grimaced.

"I can't believe she *likes* that douchebag!"

"It just seems a little *old* to go out with some guy who's still in *high* school, I mean. . ." Janie rolled her eyes at the window.

"Whatever." Jake slouched into his seat, landed his hand at twelve o'clock, and shrugged. "It's not like there aren't going to be plen-ty of hot girls at this thing. *Hey.*" He grinned and glanced his sister's way, waiting for her full attention. "Is it true Gabrielle Good's gonna be there?"

Janie leaned against the vibrating passenger door and regarded her pink terry tracksuited brother in disgust.

"Oh shit," he said, to her surprise. *Was he actually going to apologize?* But then she noticed the impressed expression on his face, the encroaching thump of a hip-hop base, a gesticulating valet, mini-flashlight in his hand . . . and held her breath.

"We're here."

Gabrielle Good (er than you)

I'M MORE OF A
DO FIRST
THINK LATER
KIND OF GIRL

Janie Famish

The Girl: Gabrielle Louise Good
The Getup: Orchid pure silk tank dress with scoop neckline and pleated detail by Doo.Ri, neon pink patent platform pumps by Alexander McQueen, candy pink Trick-or-Treater handbag by POSEUR!!!

"All right, y'all!" Melissa clapped her slender tan hands, manicured as always in Paparazzi Pink, and despite the chaos of cars arriving, music thumping, cameras popping, and pulses jumping, her tiny clap won the attention of at least thirty people. For once, she only wanted the focus of five: Charlotte and Jules, looking like they'd stepped from the pages of *Vanity Fair*; Marco, adorable in the Dolce & Gabbana pink crushed-velvet tux she'd picked out; Deena, wearing completely unauthorized pink satin genie pants that would *seriously* have to be addressed later; and Emilio Poochie, flawless as always in his pink rhinestone-encrusted Harry Winston collar and matching Paparazzi polish. Pursing her Glossimer-slathered lips, the impatient diva stared at the freshly mown grass, waiting for her twenty-five nonessential listeners to lose interest. At last they looked away, resuming their excited chatter. "I want your peepers peeled for a *red 911 Porsche*," she addressed her entourage in a confidential tone. "If I miss a *second* of this thing," she paused to spring a warning finger, "I'm holding y'all responsible, ya hear?"

"Ch'ere is stool you ch'ave requested, Miss Melissa," interrupted a tallish valet with piercing blue eyes and a thick Russian accent. With a stony formality ill fitting to his youth, he placed a beige plastic stool at her scintillating feet, tipped a bow, and slunk away. Melissa nodded her thanks and grasped Marco's hand, gathering the ruched skirt of her floor-length rose viscose Donna Karan goddess gown. Evan and Gabrielle were going to arrive any second, and she *demanded* the perfect, uninterrupted view. *And if the rest of these jokers got a perfect, uninterrupted view of her?* she softly grunted, mounting the stool in all her goddess-gown glory. *Then all the better.*

"Oh my lord," she gaped, eyes settling on a corner of the crowd. Clapping her hands once, she cackled. "Is he for *real*?"

Marco followed his girlfriend's twinkling gaze to the end of the drive. "Oh shit!" he doubled over, hiding his laughter in one hand and jerking his knee to his elbow. From a distance, Jake grinned, yanked the right leg of his pink tracksuit to his knee, and slowly pimp-walked his approach. Behind him, his sister rolled her eyes.

"Man." Melissa's boyfriend exuberantly bumped his fist, beaming with pride (at this point, almost everyone was laughing, even Charlotte, who tempered her capitulation with a disapproving shake of her head). Flashing a grin that could guide Santa's sleigh, Marco declared, "You got *balls*."

"I don't understand." Jules, by far the most tastefully dressed in a classic pink lightweight cotton twill Ralph Lauren suit, furrowed his handsome dark brow, gently tugging his girlfriend's arm. "What is funny?"

Charlotte's smile wavered; *that she had to explain!* "Well," she began, and Janie couldn't help but eavesdrop, wondering if at any point she'd acknowledge her hypocrisy. *Why,* she wished she had the nerve to interrupt. *Why is it when Jake intentionally wears stupid clothes, you think it's hot, and Marco gives him props? Your mom's eighties dress was ten* times *funnier than that tracksuit. And yet, oh no — God forbid I wear it.* Of course, the hypocrisy wasn't Charlotte's. It was the world's. When a girl dressed for laughs, it was like, even if a guy *did* think she was sexy, he wouldn't admit it. Meanwhile, members of her own gender reacted with that special mixture of mirth and disgust, like dressing weird was equivalent to public drunkenness. Or involuntary drooling. *It wasn't fair,* Janie decided.

"Hey . . ." A melodious voice diverted their attention. Her honey gold hair, which gleamed in gratitude from a rare shampooing, tumbled freely about her shoulders and fell to her waist. A sheerish cotton pink tie-dyed maxidress billowed about her ankles, exposing in glimpses her perfect, tanned ankles and open-toed espadrilles. Not that Janie noticed this stuff. She was too busing gawking at the guy to her left: hot pink vinyl pants, torn pink Patti Smith t-shirt, black, fuchsia-tipped mohawk. "This is Paul," Petra smiled, grasping his hand; on his thumb, a mood ring (*a mood ring?!*) gleamed.

"Omigod," Charlotte almost tittered, and immediately glanced between Paul and Janie, who fluttered her gray eyes shut, struggling to organize her horror into one actual coherent thought. *Pautra was with Pet?! No, no, wait . . . Traul was with Pépé?!*

Arcing an ebony eyebrow, Charlotte sang under her breath. "Awkward!"

"What?" Petra frowned, confused, wounded, and mostly just stoned. "Wait . . ."

"Hey . . ." Paul, who'd heard Charlotte and chose to ignore her, recognized Janie at last. "I know you."

"*Know* her?" The petite brunette folded her tiny arms over her fitted pink jacquard bodice. "Is that what badass punk rockers who still let Mommy buy their underwear are calling it these days?"

"Charlotte," Janie rasped, the bile rising in her throat. *Oh God. Of course, she'd recognized him. Of course she had!* "Don't —"

"Don't *what?*" the smaller girl gaped in exasperation and disbelief. "Come *on*, Janie. Don't let him treat you like that."

"You d-d-don't," she stammered, simultaneously swallowing and gasping for air. "It's-s-s not . . ."

"What's going on?" Petra blurted, pulsing with paranoia. Imploringly, she looked at Paul.

"Isn't it obvi, Pot-tra," Charlotte scowled, bored already. "These two went out."

"Wait, *what?*" he grimaced, staring accusingly at Janie. "No, we didn't."

"I know!" Janie grinned in this terrible, face-melting way. *I don't even like you anymore!* she wanted to scream. *Get over yourself.* The world was spinning, *actually* spinning, like that time at the Santa Monica pier when she was eight and ate too much kettle corn and rode the Ferris wheel and got off and smelled the fish-filled sea and puked on the boardwalk. Everyone was looking at her, their faces alternately baffled and appalled. *Don't cry,* she swallowed as her eyes began to burn. *Do not . . .*

"Excuse me," she whispered, pushed past her brother, who was still talking to Marco, and fled. Petra stared after her, her comprehension dawning.

"I'm *serious*," Paul insisted earnestly, touching her bare shoulder. "Petra — she's just this friend of Amelia's. I barely *know* her."

"Whatever," she grimaced, closing her tea green eyes. *Focus,* she ordered herself. But she couldn't. Her feet were blocks of static, her brain was too big for her skull, and his hand . . . his hand was a tarantula. She shivered, shrugging it off. "I'll be right back."

Paul watched in dismay as she ran, chasing after Janie. "This is funny!" some ponytailed douchebag tittered, glancing between him and his MIA girlfriend. "No?"

"Omigod!" Melissa squealed, resnatching their attention and

unknowingly saving Jules from a disciplinary shove. Marco struggled to hold her steady as she bounced precariously on her stool. "They're here!" she gasped, clapping her ring-adorned hands. "They're here!"

Pop! Pop! PoppityPOPpoppityPOPpopopop! PopPOPop!

Two impossibly long legs swung from the shining red Porsche door, and the paparazzi went ballistic. "Gabrielle!" they cried, falling over one another as the blithe blond starlet stepped to the curb and unfolded into the air, rising like a rare night-blooming flower. Bright lights pulsed at a seizure pace, delicate bulbs tinkled and smashed, and all the while Gabrielle Good exuded hand-on-hip cool, squaring her shoulders, angling her chin, and transitioning from pout to smile with such alien ease, her true mood (did she have one?) was puzzling to fathom. That is, until Evan Beverwil — beautiful and blasé in breezy pink linen — arrived at her side, and she lit up in a way that had nothing to do with cameras. With a new, teasing smile, she batted him lightly with her startlingly fresh pink handbag, and he laughed, touching the small of her back.

Her orchid pink slip dress looked cool and slippery under his hand.

"Aren't they *perfect* together?" Melissa choked up with emotion, causing Marco to give the couple a second, scrutinizing glance.

"I guess they're both blond," he shrugged.

"No, not her and *him*," she grimaced, like his idiocy caused her pain. "Her and the Trick-or-Treat — *oh* . . ."

Clattering down the ivory marble stairs that descended from the main house and wearing a strapless pink Versace mermaid gown the shade of pure rage, Vivien Ho was shimmying, shimmying her way. Her raven hair was pulled back from her face — teased, pinned, and sprayed into a rock-hard, brain-size beehive — and as she drew close, her poison gaze pricked like a sting.

"*What,*" she hissed, grabbing Melissa's elbow, "*is going on here?*"

"Nothing." Her future stepdaughter back-stepped off the stool, wrenching her arm from Vivien's death grip. Behind her, Marco set his jaw, puffing up like a bouncer.

"Nothing?" Vivien repeated, dripping with contempt. "Girl, you think I'm an idiot?"

"All right," Seedy intervened, materializing at the scene in a cool magenta Givenchy suit. A tiepin featuring a pink Mentos-size sapphire glittered at his throat. "What's going on now?"

"She's doing a celebriteaser!" his fiancée informed her future husband, indicating the flurry of cameras at the far end of the carpet. Seedy clenched his jaw, bolting his daughter with a disciplinary glare.

"I thought we discussed this."

"But it isn't fair!" Melissa reverted to her old argument.

She couldn't *help* it. "Look!" she cried, pointing to the decidedly unlit part of the carpet where the gnome-size Tila Tequila was checking her BlackBerry, a gargantuan magenta metallic east-west top-lock Ho Bag dangling from her arm. "She's doing one too!"

"Hardly," Vivien pointed out. "You're hogging all the cameras!"

"Wait," Seedy frowned, glancing between Tila and Vivien. "I thought you invited Tila 'cause you two are friends."

"Of course," she assured him. "But TeeTee's got her ego, you know?"

"TeeTee?" her younger rival repeated in disbelief, gaping at her father. "Daddy . . . she be sellin' woof tickets, and you *know* it!"

"Enough!" her father erupted. Melissa watched him press his palm to Vivien's back and clapped her mouth shut. "We'll talk about this later," he informed her sternly.

"Yeah, we will." Vivien flashed a final, triumphant look, and then, hanging off her fiancé's elbow, headed back to the house.

"It's so unfair." Melissa whimpered, folded into Marco's arms, and allowed him to rock her gently back and forth. "It's so . . . ," she began again. And stopped. Through the crook of Marco's armpit, dangling from Gabrielle's arm, she could see it. *It's so worth it,* she realized, melting into a smile.

"You're doing good, baby!" she called, springing off her boyfriend's body. Quickly, she remounted the stool, keeping her hand on his shoulder for balance and following her precious little one with an anxious, emotional gaze. "You're doing so good!"

Marco watched in amazement as, bursting with pride, she blew the shiny pink bag a kiss.

PINK

OR SWIM...

The Girl: Miss Paletsky
The Getup: Candy pink strapless jacquard dress with pleat detail and sweetheart neckline by REDUX: Charles Chang-Lima, fuchsia patent leather bow-front flats by Miu Miu, scrunchie: confiscated

Bit by bit, the burbling crowd drifted up the polished concrete stairs and siphoned slowly through the main entrance to the modern glass-and-concrete cliff-side house. It seemed to take an eternity for the pink carpet to clear, but when it did, it seemed to do so in the instant. Twilight illuminated the consequences: the trampled lawn, strewn with crumpled foil wrappers, grill-marked hors d'oeuvre skewers, plastic glasses sour with champagne, lipstick-stained cigarette butts, and the pink carpet, stippled with stiletto marks, littered with stray sequins, one bent peacock-feather earring, and occasional crumbles of mud. Hip-hop still blasted from human-size speakers, with no one save a few guards to hear it. The overall effect was eerie, as though the guests had not slowly moved indoors but had been abducted, all at once, by a UFO.

The inside of the estate was a different story.

The largest room on the first floor had been cleared out and transformed into what can only be called a pink-frosted palace. On either side of eight French doors, pulled back and tied in blush-pink silk ribbon, curtains of roses, *real* roses in pinks of every shade, cascaded to the polished white marble floor. In the center of the room, at the top of a triple-tiered white granite fountain, an ice-sculpted Cupid poised his arrow and bow; beneath his frosted feet, water gently trickled and swirled, stirring into motion a fleet of floating pink candles. Still more candles lined the marble mantels and side tables, the tiny flames dancing as if in competition with the boutique chandeliers, which twinkled and twinkled with rose-colored crystal. If twinkling wasn't your thing, then indoor trees offered shade, their leafy branches strung with gilded birdcages, where baffled pink parakeets twittered and hopped. Dainty round tables dressed in palest pink linen offered more pink flowers — tidy bouquets of peonies, hyacinth, and tulips — but they were overlooked for greater pink delights. On one table, savory prosciutto-wrapped melon and smoked salmon sandwiches. On another, shrimp cocktails, tuna tartar, and piles upon piles of pink caviar. And then there were sweets: pink lemonade cupcakes and sour cherry meringues, strawberry shortcakes and poached pink pear delight, crystal dishes of pastel pink candy-covered chocolates, pink embossed truffles by French chocolatier Richart, and (for fun) a glittering pink pyramid of chickadee Peeps.

In the corner of the room, on a polished pink grand piano, Miss Paletsky performed. Not that anybody heard. All around her people laughed, confided, flirted, and schmoozed — the more pink grapefruit martinis they drank, the louder they got. She didn't mind. Seedy Moon had already stopped by to thank her, a beaming smile on his face. Unthinkingly, she thanked him for thanking her, and he laughed, his eyes settling briefly on her face.

"You look . . ." He laughed again and left without finishing, walking close to the piano, keeping his hand on it until, at last, he let go. *He's drunk,* she surmised. *He put his hand there for balance.* And yet, and *yet* . . . something in the gesture, the slow slide of his fingers, felt like a caress. *Stop fantasizing,* she chastised herself, and sternly resumed her playing. But every time she looked up from the board, the memory bubbled back, and she found herself blushing with happiness.

Of all pinks in the room, that was the purest.

Charlotte Beverwil's was the pissiest.

"Tell me this isn't happening," she breathed, on the opposite side of the crowded room. "Jules," she snipped, shooting darts that put Cupid's to shame, "is that *piano* woman wearing the same dress as me?"

Her ponytailed paramour glanced up from his plate of miniature raspberry tarts and swallowed. "She *is,*" he concurred, shaking his slick raven head in disbelief. If he and Charlotte had one thing in common, it was following fashion code. "But she" — his lovely, full lips turned down in distaste — "she is like a cheap rhinestone on a child's dirty Barbie shirt. *You,*" he stressed, "are the ruby."

"I don't believe you," Charlotte hissed. "It's humiliating and you know it."

With a reluctant cringe, the handsome exchange student nodded. *He knew.*

"I'm going over there to get a better look," she groused,

chlorine green eyes still riveted to the enemy, and handed Jules her half-empty champagne flute. "I'll be right back."

It took eighteen excuse me's, thirteen thanks, and seven sorry's to make it through the crowd, and only one word — *no!* — to identify her enemy. First, she froze, eyes wide with disbelief, and then, coming to, turned frantically to escape.

"Charlotte!" Miss Paletsky stopped her in her tracks. The French wench cringed, composing herself, then turned around with an air of surprise.

"Miss Paletsky!" she sang, click-clacking toward the polished pink Steinway grand. "I didn't see you."

"Oh." The teacher squinted, reached for her octagon eyewear, and slipped the glasses on, snapping Charlotte's dress into focus. "Oh," she murmured in a different tone, the smile wobbling on her face. At least they were wearing different shoes, she noted — her student's small feet flaunted the fuchsia lizard-embossed platform Dior pumps Mr. Pelligan had insisted *she* wear. Thank God, she'd refused. She could only play piano comfortably in flats, a point Mr. Pelligan finally, after a long, bitter struggle, conceded.

"I know!" The sixteen-year-old brunette laughed, valiantly pushing through the awkwardness. "Isn't this *funny*?"

"Poor Charlotte," Miss Paletsky clucked with sympathy, recovering her smile. "You *must* know, it was Mr. Pelligan who insists

TONIGHT
Miss Paletsky performs
Outfit in B (yootiful!)
by
Charles Chang-Lima

Janie farrish

I wear. Even though, I *know* . . . on me it looks so stewpid. But on you!" She sighed her happy approval. "Beautiful."

"Oh . . ." Charlotte breathed, melting with affection. "*Thank* you."

At her student's charming immodesty, the young teacher laughed.

"I *meant*, thank you for talking to Mr. Pelligan," Charlotte quickly clarified with a blush. "That other stuff, I mean, *thank* you, but, you know . . . you look pretty too!"

"Enough," Miss Paletsky shook her head in embarrassment, but Charlotte could tell she appreciated it. *And the thing was,* she thought, discarding Jules's rhinestone critique, *it was true.* Without the distraction of so much old pleather and cheap polyester, Miss Paletsky had a pretty hot bod goin' on. Her chestnut hair, customarily clipped back into a frayed pony, shone from its stylish trim and expensive blowout, dropping cleanly from a deep side-part, and swinging to her bare shoulders. Her makeup was flawless, her pink pearl pendant faultless. *If only we could do something about those glasses,* the budding style maven sighed. *And the please-like-me smile.*

"So, what do you think of this party?" she asked, sliding in next to her teacher on the bench. "If you ask me," she confided, "it's a little *gauche.*"

"I know, isn't it *wonderful?*" Miss Paletsky sighed to Charlotte's deep astonishment. *Did she seriously not know the meaning of gauche? Wasn't that, like, not knowing the meaning of apple? Or me?* "Did you get your gift bag?" the oblivious teacher continued to gush, indicating the shiny magenta bag just above her keyboard. "There are so many things, and a pink *nano*!"

"*Seriously?*" Charlotte replied, managing to shake off her Socratic spell. But she could only feign enthusiasm for a nano for so long. "So," she smiled, and deftly changed the subject. "Do you think you'll have an engagement party?"

"Oh . . ." Miss Paletsky gripped her face with one hand, covering her mouth, and stared down at her lap. Briskly, she shook her head. "No."

"Oh," Charlotte swallowed, flushing at her social gaffe. *God . . . how does Janie* do *this all day?* "It's just, I thought . . ."

"Oh, I was," the Russian pianist assured her, glancing up and endeavoring a brave smile. "Just not anymore."

"Oh," she nodded, searching for the right words. "I'm sorry."

"No, no!" Miss Paletsky pushed some air from between her lips, waving her garishly manicured hand. "Is *good* thing, *don't* worry." She smiled, patting her student's jacquard-covered knee. "You should never be with someone you don't love," she advised, still smiling. But her brown eyes were glassy. "There is *never* a good excuse. *Never.*"

Charlotte solemnly nodded, both wondering at her teacher's words and allowing them to sink in. And then, just beyond Miss Paletsky's glossy chestnut hair, and seated on a low white couch by the window, she saw him — flanked by female admirers. They tugged at his pink terry sleeve and demanded his attention, dissolving into *peals* of spastic laughter every time he opened his mouth. And even though he looked slightly bored (his admirers were, after all, six years old), Charlotte had to admit.

She was beside herself with jealousy.

"I'll be right back." She excused herself from Miss Paletsky, rising in a stupor from the lacquered pink bench. Her heart pounding, she pushed through the crowd without speaking. She didn't need words; sensing her urgency, people simply parted, watching her with amused, unsympathetic eyes. When, at last, she spotted Jules, he was exactly where she left him. He'd set her champagne flute on the mantel by a candle and was running his hand through the flame with unflagging, childlike interest. The flickering light imbued his face in gold.

He was more beautiful that ever.

"Jules," she spoke, surprising him, and he flinched, burning his finger.

"Yes?" he turned, sucking the burn, and she paused. She couldn't break up with him *now*. Not with his finger in his mouth. Not when he looked like a hamster at the waterspout. It wasn't *right*.

At last, he removed the holdup and frowned, examining the damage.

"The thing is . . . ," she began carefully. His finger drifted upward, headed once more for the mother ship, and in a burst of panic, she blurted, *"I can't be with you anymore!"*

He froze — amber eyes wide, full mouth agape — his wounded fingertip just touching his lower lip. He looked less like a hamster than a cover girl, coyly posed to push a new lip-plumper. But then his finger fell, his mouth clapped shut . . .

And he looked like a just-been-dumped boyfriend.

— "I'm sorry," she exhaled, touching his elbow. And she *was*. But more profoundly, she was free.

The Ghost: Janie Farrish
The Getup: None of it matters now

It would go down in history as the most humiliating night of her life. She knew that much. It would go down in history as the most humiliating night. In life. *Period.* She wanted nothing more than to get the hell out of there, to crawl into bed and never come out again — but she couldn't. Jake had the keys, and Jake was inside, and she . . . she was outside, crouched against the large wall behind a thick camellia hedge. Filmy gray cobwebs clung to the leaves, some of them dark and glossy, most of them dusty and dull. A few feet away, a garden hose hissed at the wall, leaking water into dirt that smelled metallic and cold, like pennies. Every two minutes, wobbling in place, she uprooted her heels from the dampening soil, and thought: *This is what it's like to be buried.*

It was an odd kind of comfort. Unless she thought she was dead, it was like . . . she seriously wanted to die. If she was alive, not only had *it happened* (the look on his face, the look on *her* face, stricken, then scornful, confused, then suspicious; and God, her *own* face, ugly, unhinged, blotchy, and sputtering) but *continued* to happen, the toxic black fallout of her little white lie. How could she ever *explain* it? Even to herself, it was unexplainable. Except that of *course* she'd wind up like this; she was that kind of person, miserable because she deserved it, and mystifying in the worst possible way, like dirty underwear left in the street. Oh, but if she was dead! Then it was *over*. She was but a kindly spirit now, gazing through the sepulchral leaves and smiling at the living — their exaggerated joys, their petty sorrows! *Does anybody realize what life is while they're living it? Every, every minute?*

But something always wrenched her back, unearthing her from the grave like a bulldozer. The bad thing about hiding: it protects, but also traps. At one point, Paul and Petra walked outside, and oblivious to the swarming crowd of guests, talked intensely on the lawn. At another, Gabrielle pulled Evan by the hand, leading him to the pool. But when Paul and Petra made up, kissing — *literally* — in the moonlight, she had nowhere to run. When Gabrielle kicked a splash of pool water, shrieking with delight as Evan, his pant leg soaked, chased her back inside, she had no choice but to sit there, alone with her heartbeat, and cry. She wasn't dead at all, she realized. She was alive.

Horribly, painfully, absurdly alive.

By the time she lifted her face from her snot-slicked knees, half the deck had cleared. For whatever reason, the raucous party chatter had reduced to a polite, low-level murmur, and people were heading inside. She gulped down her sobs and sniffed, watching with interest, startling now and then when stiff petticoats brushed against the bush. A few moments later, she heard a snap — the glass door sliding shut — and held her breath, waiting for another sound, her ears pricked and alert. Nothing. She counted to thirty. Still nothing. Her heart pounded. Had everybody left? Was she *stuck* here? Why hadn't Jake looked for her? *Why?* What would she do? Stay here until morning to be sniffed out by Emilio Poochie? Until Melissa came down in her silk Prada pajamas?

In a burst of panic and crackling twigs, she scrambled from the hedge, briskly brushed her naked knees, and staggered a short distance across the lawn. Maybe Jake was waiting for her out front? Then, at the deck, she stopped, gazing into the bright glass windows. Inside, the rosy pink room was packed, full of beaming, laughing faces. All at once, they lifted their arms, champagne flutes in the air. Voices swelled, but she couldn't make out the words.

Whoops.

Still, now that she was out, the hedge held less appeal. Trusting no one would notice her, she tugged off Georgina's pink satin Yves Saint Laurent heels and crept across the slate-tiled deck, sitting beside the pool. Her designer dress was so short and tight, she had no choice other than to sit sidesaddle, knees bent to one side, propped up by one palm. Brushing her knees more thoroughly, she gazed into the midnight water. Rather than dip below a border, like most pool surfaces she'd seen, this surface brimmed to the top, as if the deck itself had gradually turned to liquid. Because the pool was built on a cliff, the effect was particularly breathtaking on the opposite side. The pool didn't end so much as vanish — dark water dissolving into the huge night sky. If not for a sudden smattering of stars, you could imagine it went on forever. Wouldn't that be nice? If she could just slip into the water and swim out to the stars? If all she had to do to leave this party, this glass house, these dark hills, was plunge into the cool, opaque water and *swim*, only occasionally rising for breath, until finally she'd check behind her shoulder and the earth would be far away, bobbing behind her like a bright blue buoy.

A sudden burst of chatter wrenched her from her thoughts. Reluctantly, she looked up and her heart, which had finally mellowed into something approaching peace, rattled awake and careened against her chest, urging her to flee.

But like an elephant in a tar pit, she was stuck.

"Hey," he called from the open door, his hand still gripping the handle. "You're missing the toast."

"It's fine," she told him, surprised at her voice. It sounded exhausted. And mean. "I'm fine," she waved a bit, attempting a different tone. Nope. Just as bad.

Evan nodded and stepped forward, sliding the door shut behind him. She blinked, confused.

He was coming toward her.

"Nice night," he commented, thrusting his hands into his pockets. Blood rushed into her face, and her ears throbbed *shhhhhh*, like the sound of static or the inside of a shell. He was standing right beside her. Oh God, he was *sitting* right beside her, displacing the air, which was both warm and cold. "Cool pool," he noted, training his chlorine green eyes on the horizon. In her restricting dress, Janie awkwardly rocked forward to hug her knees. *He knew.* Of *course* he knew. Was that why he was out here? To gingerly tell Janie Farrish, girl psycho, he was longer in need of her tattoo services? Or perhaps to clarify, in case her *particular* brand of crazy extended past Paul Elliot Miller to include other boy innocents, like himself, that they'd *definitely* never dated? In fact, he'd inform her, he was dating Gabrielle Good. In fact, he'd confess, they were in love.

"Where's Gabrielle?" she asked, and inwardly cringed. So much for aloof, breezy interest.

"I don't know." He shrugged as if he couldn't care less.

"She seemed cool," she added, hoping to push him to admit what she already knew: *They were perfect for each other.* "Don't you think?"

"I don't *know,*" he repeated, running his hands through his mop of sandy gold-brown hair. "What about you? Where's your *boy-friend?*"

Janie stared, overcome by the miraculousness of his ignorance. She'd just assumed everybody knew. And if *everybody* didn't know, then — at the very least — Evan did. Wouldn't Charlotte have said something? She considered responding, "Oh, we broke up," and then flinched, appalled for even *thinking* it. *There's only one way out of this,* she told herself, squeezing her eyes shut. A short breath later, she spat it out.

"I made him up."

He looked at her with a hesitating half-smile, like a person who thinks he recognizes someone only to realize *nope* — not who he'd thought. All she could do was shrug. Then, to her astonishment, he laughed. It wasn't the *best* laugh in the world — more *wow, you're freakin' weird* than *aren't you a card* — but a laugh none-theless.

"So . . ." Unable to look at him since confessing her pathetic lie, she leaned forward, drawing a line in the tepid water. "Did you decide which tattoo you wanted?"

"Nah," he said, hugging his knee. She could hear his clothes crease, shifting on his skin. "I actually think tattoos are kind of dumb."

"What?" She started to laugh and stopped, startled by the sound. Behind the hedge, she'd believed so intensely she'd never laugh again that, having done so, she felt ashamed. "So, then," she continued in a more blasé tone, "why'd you ask me to design one?"

"I don't know." He shrugged, picking at his dark coral flip-flop. His sandy blond hair swept across his eyes; when he blinked, it twitched. "Just wanted an excuse to chill with you, I guess."

She searched his profile — was this some kind of joke? He glanced up from his foot and smiled, but she only stared, too stunned to return it. With an exaggerated bob of his eyebrows, he returned to his flip-flop, and her stomach flopped, fluttering with regret. She was vaguely aware of an opportunity lost, but what? Desperate to recapture the moment, but why?

"You have attached earlobes," she blurted. *Noooo!* Her dignity howled its last, dying breath. First the I-made-up-my-boyfriend confession, now *this*? Seriously, what was *wrong* with her? "It's a recessive trait," she blathered on like a mental patient. "Attached lobes are recessive and unattached lobes are dominant. Like *my* lobes." Her eyes glazed. Something about referring to your own lobes. Something about the *word*.

Lobes.

"Yeah, I understand the genetics," he assured her. "It's just . . ." He tugged his ear and frowned. "You're *sure* mine are attached?"

Double-checking felt way too intimate. Staring at his calloused thumb, she adjusted her super-short hemline and slowly nodded. "Yeah."

"Man," he sighed, sitting back on his hands. He shook his tousled head, blowing some air between his perfect rose-wax lips. "I'm recessive."

She laughed. "You make it sound so serious."

"It *is* serious," he insisted. And then, in a tone meant to communicate both anguish and acceptance: "My earlobes are pussies."

"What?" she shrieked. He was trying his best not to smile, and failing. "You're earlobes are not" — despite herself, she lowered her voice, kind of like her mother when she said "diarrhea" — *"pussies."*

"Ah, man. Don't . . ." He winced in mock distaste. "Don't patronize me."

"I am not patronizing you," she beamed.

"You are," he insisted, and turned to face her more closely. "And you know why? 'Cause you know you're dominant."

"Oh my God . . ." She flicked some water off her fingers, rolling her eyes.

"See? You can't even take me seriously."

"Dude!" she sputtered, and — before she could think it through — pushed his shoulder. "It's my *earlobes* that are dominant. Not my entire being."

"Yeah, well . . . you're wrong."

"You *actually* think I dominate you," she said with a self-conscious smirk, like, *Thanks for making me say the stupidest thing in the world,* and bobbed her eyebrows, cuing him to respond. But he just looked at her. And this time she didn't look away. In the corner of her eye, she saw him rubbing his knee, wiping off miniscule grains of gravel. Her mouth twitched, begging for a joke, for something to *say* — but then his hand left his knee, and she forgot how to think. He was brushing back a strand of her hair; he was hooking it gently behind her ear. Tiny thrills branched across her face and neck, electrifying her veins. She'd never felt so awake. She'd never felt so completely out of it. She'd dreamed of this moment a million times — to have a boy brush her hair from her face, to hook it gently behind her ear; it was the most romantic thing in the world, even more than kissing because it required *nothing* from her: she wouldn't be able to mess it up. He did it again, and this time lingered at her ear, slowly tracing the edge, his brow furrowed with boyish concentration. At last, he found it — the softest part — compressing it gently between his forefinger and thumb. She willed herself to look at him, to actually sustain eye contact, but, except for that one time, didn't have the courage. Instead, blushing into her lap, she thought about the big bang — how a tiny speck of nothing became an infinite every-thing — not only stars and planets but, like, *time*. And *light*. And *space*. It had always seemed so impossible; now, it made perfect sense. The mystery was something else. The mystery was *when*.

How do you choose your moment to explode?

And then she looked up. For no reason at all. Except, she found out, to kiss him. So, they were kissing.

They were kissing.

The Gangsta: Seedy Moon
The Getup: Eat it or wear it

They were kissing. *Y'all see that?* Everything cool. Never mind it
felt about as natural as kissing a coatrack. Or his cousin Malaika
in the second grade. But if he could get through a kiss, then things
were *all right*. That seaweed ingredient? Just a coincidence. Vee
wasn't Swamp Thing, she was *Miss Thang*. Which was why, in just
a few minutes, in front his family, friends, and Tila Tequila, he
was gonna get up and *say* so. Everyone else had made their damn
toasts, why shouldn't he?

Vivien squeezed his hand and turned, disappearing into the
scintillating crowd.

"Hey!" He beckoned to a passing server, flashing a winning
smile. The server, a jowly older dude with a jutting lower lip,
hairy-ass forearms, and big ol' baby head, sauntered over with his
tray. *Huh,* Seedy thought. *So much for L.A. waiters all being hot-to-
trot actor types.* "Let me at that champagne, brother," he laughed,
reaching for a glass.

Baby Head did not laugh back.

"Not really into this shizz," the rapper explained to the server's evident boredom (were his eyebrows that permanently raised
type, or what?), "but I gotta make this toast, so, you know, got to
clink my fork on something. . . ." He finally trailed off, surrendering to the server's religiously unamused stone-face. What was *with*

this dude? "Man," he ventured, scratching his shaved head. "You all right?"

The server shrugged. "Is there anythin' ailse I can ch'elp?"

"Nah." Seedy took a swig of champagne and shook his head slowly. "I'm cool."

The server nodded; he and the champagne flutes continued on their way. Sliding a polished fork off a nearby table, Seedy watched after him.

He'd have to look into this catering company.

Clattering his fork to the side of his glass, he greeted the glittering crowd, walking backward. "Spuh-*eech!*" Tiombé, the backup vocalist on Lil' Miss Chang, cried out, raising her fist. Within seconds, every guest was his, hooting and hollering and calling his name.

"See-dy! See-dy! See-dy!"

"Ah, ha-ha!" He beamed his appreciation, mounted the polished marble stairs that led to the next room, and scanned the hundreds of gleeful, shining faces. *"Vee,"* he bellowed in a mock-authoritative baritone, eliciting an inevitable high-pitched *whooooo!!!* followed by a cackling round of applause. By the wall of rose curtains, Vivien hid her face in her hands, shaking her elaborately coiffed head. "Get up here, baby!" Seedy warned, and she lowered her hands to her mouth, gazed at her friends with bright, embarrassed eyes, and then surrendered, lifting up her pink chiffon mermaid skirt and trotting gaily through the crowd. In seconds, she was at Seedy's side, bowing with laughter and clapping her hands.

"As y'all know by now!" Seedy began, and then smiled, waiting for his audience to simmer down. "As you all *know*!" He began again, and this time the volume took a dip. "I am a songwriter."

A smattering of laughter convulsed through the room. *Of course they knew. He was Seedy Moon!* The hip-hop giant took a deep breath and cleared his throat. The crowd was pretty quiet now — just a sea of expectant faces. A sea, you know. Like where seaweed was from. No, wait. That wasn't right.

"We rhymers be *trippin'*!" he continued, soliciting another round of laughter — a little quieter this time. He rubbed his chin and frowned. Had he forgotten a line, or . . . ? Looking up, he noticed his daughter — she was standing by the piano, her forehead furrowed with worry. Beside her, Lena squeezed her shoulder and, suddenly aware of his attention, nodded once, encouraging him to go on.

"As y'all know . . ."

"Baby!" With an embarrassed smile to her audience, Vivien linked his arm and leaned in close, hissing through her teeth. *"What do we all know?"*

Lightly twisting free from her arm, Seedy stepped back, searching her familiar face. "Did you . . . ," he began in a low voice. "Did you do it?"

"Do what?" she whispered, nervously aware of the crowd, now burbling with curiosity and concern.

"Melissa's contest," he replied, still searching her face.

"What are you talking about?" she frowned, dropping his arm. "Are you messin' with me?"

"LIAR!" A voice boomed, and sent seismic swells of wrath across the room. The multitude of guests turned to the back of the room. Miss Paletsky gasped in horror.

"*Yuri!*" she cried, gaping at a squat, barrel-shaped cater-waiter stationed at the other end of the piano. "What are you doing ch'ere?"

"You think I don't find out? You think I am *byeaz oom yets*? YOU!" He whirled on his heel, pointed a trembling, hairy-knuckled finger up at Seedy, and glared across the room. "You think you can ch'ave double life, eh?" He spat on the floor. "Why don't you face me like *man?*"

"*Gloo*pei slepits!" Lena erupted, flushed with mortification. "What do you think?" she warned, and inexplicably clutched her pink nano. "I don't call police?"

"That won't be necessary," Seedy interrupted loudly but clearly, and then, with his hardest gangsta glare, stepped down the stairs. One by one, his people moved aside, parting for him like the Red Sea, and Yuri hacked a noisy cough, pressing a napkin to his moistened, unimpressed lips. Beads of sweat glistened on his skull and dampened the buttoned white shirt that strained, against all odds, to contain his pendulous gut. In contrast, Seedy was compact, svelte — a muscle-bound machine. The Russian crumpled his pink napkin into his fist, dropped it on the floor, and faced him with a down-turned mouth. Seedy had to give him some respect. For a dude in his shape, he was balls-to-walls *crazy*.

"Say *chaas!*" he barked, snapping his fingers. A few unlucky guests yelped as Yuri's *Bratva*, disguised this whole time as servers and valets, emerged from within the crowd and roughly shouldered them aside, among them Nikolai Mogilevich, Melissa's steely-eyed stool bearer, and Boris "Bobo" Balagula, otherwise known as Baby Head. The men revered Yuri; in Moscow, he belonged to the *Vory v zakone*, an elite band of criminals existing in Russia since the days of the Tsar from whom Yuri was *also* (he'd emphatically declared over lunch at Canter's Deli, a shred of sauerkraut quivering on his lip) *directly descended*. Now, since 1991, he continued his shady dealings at the Copy & Print store on Fairfax, selling black market plasma screens, cell phones, Louis Vuitton, Prada, and purebred baby dogs out of a storage basement. All his men were in on it, except, of course, for Nikolai, whom he'd hired to work the copy machine.

As soon as Seedy became aware of Yuri's encroaching entourage, he jerked back his chin, exhaling sharply through his nostrils. Within seconds, the rapper was flanked by his main Moon men: Harlem, G-Nugz, Reginald, and *the Man from K-Town* who, with a heavy sigh, reluctantly put down his half-eaten Peeps.

Now, they were locked into a face-off: thug against thug, posse against posse.

"You wanna do this thing?" Seedy flared, folding his extremely cut arms across his broad chest. Young Nikolai turned to Yuri with beseeching ice blue eyes.

"What kind of night shift is this?" he complained in Russian. "I want to work Xerox, not get my ass kicked by a bunch of gang members."

"The boy has a point, Yuri," Baby Head grumbled, also in Russian. "Maybe twenty years ago . . . but now?" He shook his head. "I am too old."

"Cowards," Yuri muttered, but you could see it in his face: he too had given up. Turning to Seedy, he pushed out his lower lip. "We will not fight."

"Good," Seedy stonily replied, still folding his arms. "My man Reg'll escort y'all outside."

"Right thith way," gap-toothed Reginald lisped, ushering them to the door. Again the crowd parted (Miss Paletsky turned to the wall, closed her eyes, and pressed her knuckles to her mouth) and the four men shuffled by, staring at the floor, enduring their Walk of Shame. As they passed a table, Yuri noticed for the first time a platter of Richart truffles. In the shadow of the platter, lying on the table, another truffle, half eaten, tilted on its side. The sight of it lying there mutilated, rejected, filled him with something like compassion. Gently, he picked it up.

"You better put that back," Reginald cautioned — and it was all the Russian could take. His steely eyes flashed.

"Oigah!"

Seedy's henchman flinched, flew a hand to his stung forehead, and wiped off a smear of chocolate. "Fool," he looked up from his chocolate-stained fingers in disbelief. "You juthst *bean* me?" The Russian licked his lips, readying his response, and Reginald frowned, reaching for a heavy crystal bowl. Yuri roared as an arsenal of hard pink candy hearts hailed down on his hard pink head, clattering hysterically to the hard marble floor. Reddening with rage, Baby Head palmed an enormous double-layered pink-frosted coconut cake, grunted a small step forward, and smashed it into Reginald's unsuspecting face.

Needless to say, all chaos broke loose.

A jaw-clenched Seedy Moon raced through the crowd and, at the last possible moment, lunged, thudding his full weight into Lena's portly tormentor; the crowd collectively gasped as together they careened across the overdressed table. Seedy hapkido-pinned his struggling opponent into place, grinding fistfuls of strawberry shortcake into his sputtering, ruddy face. With a flap of his burly arms, Yuri scooped frosting into his thick hands, clapping it explosively to his rival's ears. The table tipped over with a crash, tumbling the two men to the floor, burying them both in an avalanche of crushed cakes, finger sandwiches, silverware, and plates. All around them, people pushed and shrieked, desperate to evade a fatal dry-cleaning bill. At another table, Baby Face and G-Nugz went at it, wrestling in an oozing swamp of pink caviar, stuffing icy shrimp down their shirts, shrieking like two girls at a pool. Young Nikolai ducked for cover, cowering behind a potted indoor tree, firing sour cherry meringues like grenades. A slimy slice of smoked salmon slapped Vivien across the face and she screamed, clawing for the ballroom door. At the relatively pristine piano, Melissa consoled a sobbing Tila Tequila (who'd just been Carrie'd in chilled strawberry gazpacho), surreptitiously wiping her salmony fingers on the MySpace diva's convulsing back. As Miss

Paletsky grabbed her hand, pulling her toward the poolside exit with everyone else, pink parakeets panicked, screeching inside their cages, watching in horror as their Peeps brethren scattered across the floor, crushed in moments by the stampede of heels.

And all the while, as the situation spiraled out of control, Jules watched curiously from a relatively quiet corner of the expansive room. *I do not think this would happen in Switzerland,* he frowned as the now decapitated Cupid lurched through the air and crashed through the rose-draped window, chased by a flock of shrimp projectiles. Something hard skidded across the floor, thwacking to a stop at his shiny dress shoe. He bent to his knees, picking it up. A tiny pink candy heart. He looked up, observing again this impossible American pandemonium. He abhorred food fights; they were worse than boorish; they flew in the face of basic humanity. *Hundreds of thousands of people going hungry in the world,* he thought, flicking from his cheek a gob of pale pink frosting. *How do they justify it?* And yet, there with the miniature heart's weight in his palm, he couldn't deny the tiniest urge to throw it. He sighed, disturbed by this new development — it was so *unlike* him. But maybe that was precisely the point. His heart was broken, and, well, he wanted to do something as unlike him as possible, to get away from himself — if only for a moment. He scanned the horde for Charlotte, and finding her nowhere, sighed. Closing his eyes, he pressed the hard, sweet heart to his lips.

With all his might, he threw it.

December 13, 3:42 p.m.

Fellow Winstonians, Fashionistas, and Fabulazzi:

Unless y'all be livin' under a twenty-six-carat rock, you heard what went down at my crib the other night. Well, as someone who was there, *not to mention a central player*, I'd like to set the record straight. Everything you heard so far?

Is true.

Our family thanks you for respecting our privacy during this difficult time.

Hahahahhahaha!!!! Just *kiddles*, ma *bibbles*!

NOW FOR THE MOTHER MCMUFFIN FACKS:

1. Vivien Ho, my dad's soon-to-be-very-ex-fiancée, stands accused of sabotaging the Poseur contest. (Do not even get me *started* on this!)

2. Sometime during our off-the-chain Russian mafia food brawl (I'm thinking we hold one every year, haha), Gabrielle Good passed out *cold*—had her fancy-pantz straight up ambulanzed to Cedars—where (along with enough Adderalic beverage to TKO a T-Rex) doctors discovered the *teensiest* bump on her precious head. Further examining revealed a tiny but mighty heart-shaped candy caught up in her hair extensions. Now she's claiming foul play, like, "I was attacked!" *Whatever*. The only thing attacking *that* girl's the e-g-o-zilla. Which is a *good* thing because . . .

3. The Treater's along for the ride! Not to beat a dead clotheshorse, but ever since Lady GaGo's incident (and the *fameulous* photo that goes with it) our baby bag's been all over *People*, *Us*, Perez, the *LA* and *New York Times*, and (coming soon!) *NYLON*. Look for us in Feb's "Fashion and Features," y'all! Oh, and if you *still* haven't gotten a Treater, best light some fire under your Fendis and get with the showgram. Ted Pelligan's sayin' the waitlist's "longer than Isabella Blow's front tooth." Yah, we dunno what that means neither, but we *think* he's saying . . .

Fashion history is in the *making*, bébés! We can *feel* it.

Yours with a cherry on top,

Melissa, Janie, Charlotte, Petra

In the words of Vladimir Fabokov,
"Think like a genius, dress like a rock star,
and speak like a child."

So what do *you* dress like, anyway?

You can be a Janie, a Charlotte, a Petra, or a Melissa . . .
or even a crazy combination of all four. (Hm . . . are you
an Ottelissaniepet?)

Whatever you design, turn the page and make their
looks your own. New York City fashion label Compai
shows you how. It's easier than one, two, um . . . spree!

CHARLOTTE'S TOTE BAG

You'll need:

1 piece of pink cotton canvas
 measuring 15.7 in. x 36.2 in.
Pins
Needle and thread
2 heart-shaped buttons
2 black satin ribbons, measuring
 1.5 in. x 15.7 in.
1 piece of zebra-printed silk, measuring
 6 in. x 15.7 in.
1 black satin ribbon, measuring
 0.5 in. x 16 in.

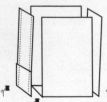

9.4" x 36.2"

4.7" x 5.5"

4.7" x 13.4"   4.7" x 13.4"

1. Cut canvas into one piece measuring 9.4 in. x 36.2 in., two pieces measuring 4.7 in. x 13.4 in., and two pieces measuring 4.7 in. x 5.5 in. Hem all raw edges.

2. Pin smaller square pieces to rectangular pieces, then top stitch bottom and sides, creating patch pockets. Decorate with heart-shaped buttons.

3. Fold larger piece in half and pin rectangular pieces to the sides, making sure pocket openings are facing upward. Stitch sides together.

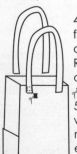

4. Pin one wide ribbon 2 in. from left side seam and 2 in. downward from top hem. Repeat on opposite side and stitch in place.

5. Repeat on other side with remaining wide ribbon, making sure the straps are even, and stitch in place.

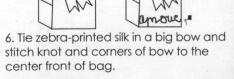

6. Tie zebra-printed silk in a big bow and stitch knot and corners of bow to the center front of bag.

7. Pin and stitch your thin ribbon carefully to the bottom corner of the bag, forming the word "amour" for a French touch.

JANIE'S DRESS

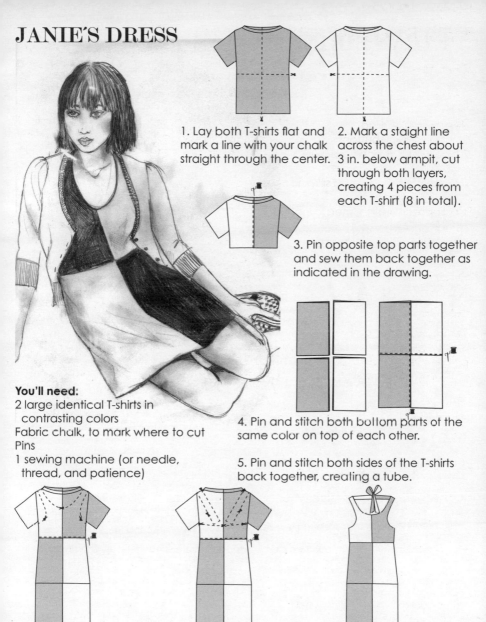

1. Lay both T-shirts flat and mark a line with your chalk straight through the center.

2. Mark a staight line across the chest about 3 in. below armpit, cut through both layers, creating 4 pieces from each T-shirt (8 in total).

3. Pin opposite top parts together and sew them back together as indicated in the drawing.

4. Pin and stitch both bottom parts of the same color on top of each other.

5. Pin and stitch both sides of the T-shirts back together, creating a tube.

You'll need:
2 large identical T-shirts in contrasting colors
Fabric chalk, to mark where to cut
Pins
1 sewing machine (or needle, thread, and patience)

6. Stitch top part together with tube, creating a checkered pattern.

7. Cut front of dress as a tank top, follow drawing where indicated with scissors.

8. Cut a diagonal line from armpit to armpit in the back of the dress.

9. Cut straps lining up with the straps you cut in front.

10. Try on and trim with scissors if needed.

PETRA'S BIKINI

1. Cut the side seams of your undies open and lay out flat on top of your T-shirt.

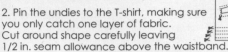

2. Pin the undies to the T-shirt, making sure you only catch one layer of fabric. Cut around shape carefully leaving 1/2 in. seam allowance above the waistband.

3. Cut across sleeves as indicated on drawing, creating two triangular pieces. Each piece should cover the size of your bust.

x4

4. Cut four 1/2 in. wide strips from bottom of T-shirt, cut one side seam open on each strip and pull to create stronger strips.

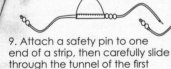

5. Fold seam allowance on both sides of your waistband downward and stitch across, creating a tunnel.

6. Attach a safety pin to one end of a strip, then slide the strip through the tunnel of the waistband. Repeat on other side with another strip, try on, and tie at sides.

7. Thread a few beads on the loose ends of strips and secure with simple knots.

8. Fold bottom of one triangular piece upward and stitch across to create a tunnel; repeat on second piece.

9. Attach a safety pin to one end of a strip, then carefully slide through the tunnel of the first triangular piece.

10. Thread a few beads onto the same strip and slide through the tunnel of the second triangular piece.

11. Thread a few beads onto loose ends and secure with simple knots.

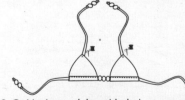

You'll need:
1 pair of old undies with a good fit; they will serve as pattern for bikini bottom
1 T-shirt, preferably black or other dark color
Pins
Needle and thread
1 safety pin
1 thrift shop necklace made of olive-size beads

12. Cut last remaining strip in two equal long strips and stitch one end to the top corner of first triangular piece, then stitch the second remaining strip to the other triangular piece.

13. Thread a few beads onto the loose ends and secure with simple knots.

MELISSA'S BUTTERFLY BELT

You'll need:
1 pair of side-cutting pliers
Thrift shop necklaces or beads of various sizes
Steel wire
Super glue or a glue gun
1 sturdy clasp, big is better
1 wide elastic, long enough to go around your
    waist with 1 in. seam allowance

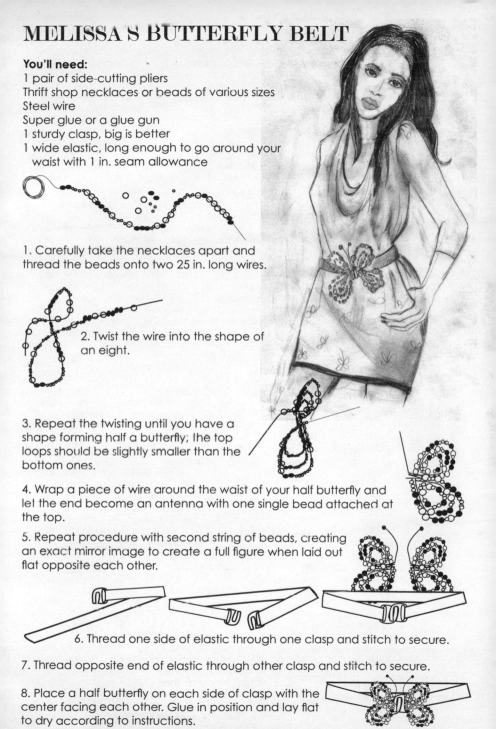

1. Carefully take the necklaces apart and thread the beads onto two 25 in. long wires.

2. Twist the wire into the shape of an eight.

3. Repeat the twisting until you have a shape forming half a butterfly; the top loops should be slightly smaller than the bottom ones.

4. Wrap a piece of wire around the waist of your half butterfly and let the end become an antenna with one single bead attached at the top.

5. Repeat procedure with second string of beads, creating an exact mirror image to create a full figure when laid out flat opposite each other.

6. Thread one side of elastic through one clasp and stitch to secure.

7. Thread opposite end of elastic through other clasp and stitch to secure.

8. Place a half butterfly on each side of clasp with the center facing each other. Glue in position and lay flat to dry according to instructions.

Being a celebrity princess isn't always a fairy tale.

Catch a glimpse behind the velvet ropes of stardom as Kaitlin Burke tries to balance being a normal sixteen-year-old with being a hot teen celebrity.

secrets OF MY HOLLYWOOD LIFE

Keep your eye out for *Broadway Lights*, coming March 2010!

Welcome to Poppy.

A poppy is a beautiful blooming red flower
(like the one on the spine of this book). It is also
the name of the home of your favorite books.

Poppy takes the real world and makes it
a little funnier, a little more fabulous.

Poppy novels are wild, witty, and inspiring.
They were written just for you.

So sit back, get comfy, and pick a Poppy.

poppy

www.pickapoppy.com